INSPIRING LEGENDS AND TALES
WITH A MORAL III

Stories From Around the World

Emerson Klees

Emerson Klees

The Human Values Series

Cameo Press, Rochester, New York

The Human Values Series

Role Models of Human Values

One Plus One Equals Three—Pairing Man / Woman Strengths:
  Role Models of Teamwork (1998)
Entrepreneurs in History—Success vs. Failure:
  Entrepreneurial Role Models (1999)
Staying With It: Role Models of Perseverance (1999)
The Drive to Succeed: Role Models of Motivation (2002)
The Will to Stay With It: Role Models of Determination (2002)

The Moral Navigator

Inspiring Legends and Tales With a Moral I: Stories From
  Around the World (2007)
Inspiring Legends and Tales With a Moral II: Stories From
  Around the World (2007)
Inspiring Legends and Tales With a Moral III: Stories From
  Around the World (2007)

Cameo Press
P. O. Box 18131
Rochester, New York 14618

Library of Congress Control Number: 2007905079

ISBN 1-891046-20-9

Printed in the United States of America
9 8 7 6 5 4 3 2 1

Preface

A moral conveys the ethical significance or practical lesson to be learned from a story. It is the principle taught by a legend or tale that portrays what is right or just. What we learn from stories with a moral is of a general or strategic nature rather than a detailed or tactical one. A moral provides a background against which to measure our attitude and behavior. The moral of a well-told story can inspire us by highlighting a virtue to emulate.

The human qualities illustrated in these legends and tales include compassion, courage, determination, humility, loyalty, perseverance, resourcefulness, and unselfishness. Some of them are familiar, such as those about Robin Hood, Noah, and Pandora; most are not as well known. The less familiar ones also deserve our attention. These stories uplift as well as entertain and show that our potential is greater than we think.

TABLE OF CONTENTS

Page No.

Introduction   6

IMMORTAL / ENDURING   *Chapter 1*   8
The Origin of Robin Hood   9
The Selection of Noah   17
The Prince Who Would Seek Immortality   20
The Blind Men and the Elephant   26
The Legend of Pandora's Box   28

NOTABLE / LOYAL   *Chapter 2*   34
Lost on Dress Parade   35
The Five Wise Words of the Guru   40
The Ditch-digger Falls into His Own Ditch   45
The Man Who Stopped Going to Church   46
The Legend of the Lute Player   48

SELF-DETERMINED / RESPONSIBLE   *Chapter 3*   52
The Green Door   53
The Cannon That Wasn't Fired   56
The King Who Would See Paradise   58
The Legend of Prince Ahmed al Kamel   60
The Legend of the Promise   75

PERSEVERING / RESOURCEFUL   *Chapter 4*   84
Diamond Cut Diamond   85
The Crumb in the Beard   88
The Three Words of Advice   92
The Legend of the White Slipper   94
The Legend of the Patient Suitor   99

INDEFATIGABLE / UNSELFISH   *Chapter 5*   105
The Legend of the Four Gifts   106
The Legend of the Stonecutter   112
How to Find a True Friend   114
The Legend of the Test   120
The Legend of the Enchanted Ring   122

Page No.

RESOLUTE / COURAGEOUS   *Chapter 6*   128
    The Little Hero of Holland   129
    Horatius at the Bridge   130
    Crossing the Rubicon   132
    Thunder Falls   133
    The Brave Three Hundred   136

EMPATHETIC / COMPASSIONATE   *Chapter 7*   138
    For Those Without Hope   139
    The Chest of Broken Glass   140
    The Slandered Sister   141
    Reconciliation by Courier   148
    The Service of Love   151

Epilogue   155

Bibliography   157

Introduction

A legend is a story or narrative, with some historical basis, often
unverifiable, handed down from generation to generation. Much of
its content may be fiction, but it has some basis in fact. A legend is
usually about people who actually lived, places that really existed,
or events that in fact occurred, all embedded in details added later
in subsequent retellings

Legends are considered authentic in the society in which they
originated. Frequently, it is difficult to determine the boundary
between fact and fiction. Folktales, initially handed down by word
of mouth, are not considered historically factual. However, the
theme of a folktale may appear in a legend or in time turn into a legend. The boundary between legends and folktales is not well
defined.

The distinction between legends and myths is described by
Richard Cavendish in the introduction to *Legends of the World*:

> Legends are on a different plane from myths, which are
> imaginative traditions about the nature and destiny of the
> world, the gods, and the human race. In some cases, as in
> the Bible, a people's account of the past begins with
> myth—the creation of the world—and then shades over
> into legends about the founding figures and leaders of the
> nation in its early history. Legends are set on the human
> rather than the divine level, and the central characters of
> legends are human beings, not gods, although they are
> often larger-than-life human beings with supernatural
> powers.

Legends become part of an inherited body of beliefs and values
that identify a society. These stories provide insight into the soci-
eties that created them. Often legends are passed on to subsequent
generations by storytellers.

Many parallels exist among the legends of the world. For
example, similarities exist in many stories of the supernatural birth
of heroes, including those in which one or both parents were gods.
Other similarities are found in the dangers that confronted many of
the heroes of legends as children. In the Greek legend of the

Pleiades, for example, the seven daughters of Atlas were changed into stars. In a parallel Iroquois Indian legend, seven young Indian children became a constellation called Oot-kwa-tah by the Iroquois.

These legends and tales are inspiring. They remind us that our lives do not necessarily have to be small lives, and that if we reach out, we can achieve much more than our perceived limitations allow us. These stories not only teach us about moral values, they provide us with examples of behavior to emulate or in some cases to avoid, and they elevate our attitude towards life.

Chapter 1

IMMORTAL / ENDURING

I decline to accept the end of man ... I believe that man will
not merely endure: he will prevail. He is immortal, not because
he alone among creatures has an inexhaustible voice but a soul,
a spirit capable of compassion and sacrifice and endurance.

William Faulkner

The Origin of Robin Hood

Having been away from home for longer than he would have liked, Robert of Locksley returned to Barnisdale Forest on the way to his home at Outwoods, just beyond the fringes of the forest. As he walked through the broad-leafed trees of the dense forest at noon in the height of summer, Robert became aware that there were very few animals in the vicinity. Quietly he hid behind a great oak tree and looked out across a small clearing, expecting to see some of the hated foresters who kept watch over the king's deer that roamed the forest.

In 1185 Robert of Locksley was a young man of twenty-five, his face bronzed by long periods spent in his beloved forests. His eyes shone brightly in a face that was full of compassion and yet had a steely quality that had and would put many in his place. He was dressed in a green tunic of rough green cloth with a broad leather belt, which held a dagger on the right side and arrows on the left. He wore supple leather breeches, a green velvet cap, and stout leather shoes.

As Robert watched, he caught a movement out of the corner of his eye. Slowly turning his head he saw the undergrowth move as three deer entered the glade. As he watched the buck and two doe, an arrow flew out of the undergrowth and struck the first doe in the heart. The other two deer fled as the stricken doe fell to the ground. Nothing stirred. The doe's killer waited before emerging for fear that the foresters might come at any moment.

Robert looked across the glade for a full five minutes. Finally he saw a man creep out of the bushes, his knife drawn as he moved slowly across the open space toward his quarry. He was dressed in the garb of a peasant, a rope around his waist holding together his rough brown tunic. When he reached the doe he crouched down and deftly cut away the most tender portions of the carcass.

Robert made no effort to show himself. He wondered what had driven this man, whom he knew, to risk life and limb in such a reckless manner. The man wrapped the meat in a piece of rough sacking and tucked it under his tunic before making his way across the glade. Robert followed at a discreet distance and then passed the man. Robert abruptly stepped out in front of him, blocking his way.

When the man saw that his route was barred, his hand went for his knife, but when he recognized Robert he greeted him warmly.

Some of the warmth left his voice when Robert questioned his actions. The man, whom Robert recognized as Will Scarlet, explained that in "Master Robin's" absence, for that was how many referred to Robert of Locksley, Will's brother-in-law John a'Green had taken ill and died, after which Will's sister and her three children had been evicted by Sir Guy of Gisborne to fend for themselves.

The mention of Guy of Gisborne reminded Robert of his own position. He and his ancestors had held a house and 160 acres of land on a legal rent from the lords of the manor of Birkencar since the manor had been given to the lords by King William. However, the last lord of the manor, Sir Guy of Wrothsley, had bequeathed the manor and all its lands to the White Monks of St. Mary's Abbey, who especially wanted the land that Robert held since it was the most fertile and productive of all their lands.

As long as Robert paid his rent on time, however, they could not legally take possession. Nevertheless, Robert knew of the evil of Sir Guy of Gisborne and was aware that, with the connivance of the monks, he had long looked for a way to dispossess Robert, even if it meant having him falsely accused of a crime and proclaimed an outlaw. Then all Robert's possessions and lands would be forfeited. For this reason Robert was returning home. He had heard that Sir Guy of Gisborne and the abbot were plotting to seize his lands.

Robert was snapped back out of his own thoughts as Will Scarlet described all that had befallen his family. His sister had come to him with her three children but died of starvation a short time afterwards. Will Scarlet kept his oldest nephew in his own charge, and kindly neighbors had taken in the other two children. It was to feed the child that he had taken to stealing the king's meat from the forest, something he would do as long as there were deer to be had.

Robert listened to the story without interrupting. However, when Will Scarlet finished, Robert told him that he should have gone to Outwoods, where Robert's steward, Scadlock, would have provided for him. Will replied that he was aware of that, but he had not wanted to make Robert any further enemies—enemies that, he added, were at that very moment scheming against him. Will was not surprised to learn that those plans were the reason for Robert's return to Outwoods. While he was in residence there, Robert hoped that the monks and Sir Guy of Gisborne would not move against him.

Robert took Will Scarlet by the shoulder and told him to place the venison on the ground next to Robert's own bow and arrows. Will Scarlet did as he was told, although he was reluctant to put down the meat that he had risked his life to obtain. Just as he was about to question Robert, he heard the voices of two foresters coming down the path. A few moments later, with the meat and the bow and arrows safely hidden, Robert of Locksley and Will Scarlet were confronted by two burly foresters who barred their way, although one, less offensive than the other, moved aside when he recognized Robert. The other, who was called Black Hugo, continued to bar the way until he saw the steely look in Robert's eyes.

Robert and Will Scarlet passed the foresters and continued on their way out of the forest. As they climbed the hill they saw Outwoods in the distance and the village in the valley between them and Robert's home. As they walked down the hill towards the village, Will Scarlet was amazed to see his meat, along with Robert's bow and arrows, lying in the grass. Will was going to ask for an explanation when he remembered that Robert had many friends in the forest.

While Will Scarlet rushed down the hill toward the village, Robert turned back into the forest to the road that went from Barnside into Nottinghamshire. He was thinking of another reason for his return to the greenwood—his promise to protect the woman he loved as she traveled through the forest. As he hurried through the dense undergrowth, he remained alert to danger at all times, even though he knew that he was accompanied by his forest friends.

Soon Robert's thoughts turned to the woman he had loved since they had played together as children in Locksley Chase. She was Maid Marian, the fair daughter of Sir Richard FitzWalter of Malaset. Although they came from different stations—she was the daughter of an earl and he was but a yeoman—they loved each other and had sworn that they would marry no other. That day Robert was there to protect his love as she traveled from her father's castle to pay a visit to her uncle Sir Richard at Lea of Linden Lea, a short distance from Nottingham.

When Robert had traveled through the forest for over five miles, he came to a road that led to a crossroads. He moved through the thick undergrowth to a small glade and walked over to a group of sticks on the ground. To an untrained eye they looked as though they had fallen from a tree. Robert sank to his knees and inspected the twigs carefully. They provided a message from his woodland friends. The twigs told him that one knight on horseback and eight knaves on foot waited in ambush nearby. He silently crept towards their position.

Robert parted the bushes. He recognized the voice of Sir Roger de Longchamp, who had long coveted Marian and had obviously come to take her by foul means. Sir Richard FitzWalter had repeatedly refused to give his daughter's hand to that treacherous knight, the brother of the proud Bishop of Fecamp and the favorite of Duke Richard.

As Robert watched the knight on his horse, his thoughts turned to his own lineage, the one obstacle that prevented him from marrying his beloved Marian. He had heard from Stephen of Gamwell that the Locksleys had once been the lords of Huntington. He knew that the earldom and the lands of Huntington had been given to David, son of the Scottish king. He wondered how it might have been different had not his forebears risen against the Normans, only to be driven from their land, home, and title.

Robert's reverie halted as a man raced into the clearing and told Sir Roger de Longchamp that Marian was approaching on horseback with one other on horseback and the remainder of her party on foot. Immediately Sir Roger barked out a series of orders. As he listened, Robert slipped an arrow from his belt. At that moment, Maid Marian rode into view, with Walter, her father's steward at Malaset, riding beside her. As Robert watched the knight charged into the clearing with his men.

Immediately Walter rode in front of his mistress to protect her and fought off the first blow from Sir Roger de Longchamp's sword with his staff. Then Walter knocked the sword out of Sir Roger's hand, but not before Sir Roger had grabbed the reins of Marian's horse. One of the knight's men knocked Walter from his horse. As Walter lay unconscious, Sir Roger began to drag Marian's horse towards him. Suddenly he fell headlong to the ground, the shaft of a arrow jutting out of his right eye through the narrow slit in his helmet.

When Sir Roger de Longchamp fell heavily to the forest floor, the fighting stopped. One of his men went over to his body and withdrew the arrow from his eye. He signalled that there was only one attacker and sent the men to find him, when an arrow streaked through the air and struck him in the heart. Since the arrow had come from the opposite side of the path, the men assumed that there were more archers. They turned and fled.

When the men had gone, Robert came out of the woods and walked up to Marian. She offered him her hand and thanked her "Sweet Robin" for saving her from the clutches of Sir Roger de Longchamp. She predicted that the knight's death would cause Robert problems, because Sir Roger's powerful and evil friends would try to avenge him. Robert helped Walter back into his saddle and led them to safety.

Robert guided the party off the road and along paths known only to him and his woodland friends. As they penetrated deep into the greenwood, only Marian and Walter were unafraid. The others grew increasingly anxious that they would be attacked by the spirits believed to live in the heart of the forest.

When the party reached the edge of the forest about a mile from the castle at Linden Lea, two knights galloped over to them, Sir Richard at Lea, Marian's uncle, and his companion, Sir Huon de Bulwell. They thanked Robert for his timely intervention in ridding their land of one vile knight. They expressed concern that Robert might not live long enough to rid them of the rest of the wicked horde who resided at the castle of Wrangby, also known as the Evil Hold.

Robert stayed at Linden Lea with Sir Richard and Lady Alice. During the day they hunted with hawks or chased wild boar in the forest; at night they were entertained by minstrels or played chess. On the fourth morning Robert went into the woods to shoot birds and saw his friend Ket the Trow, who showed himself only when he had news to tell. Although Ket the Trow was a full-grown man, he was not taller than a medium-sized youth of thirteen or fourteen; nevertheless, he had strong arms and legs and a broad chest and shoulders.

Ket the Trow told Robert that he had followed the men who had fled after Sir Roger de Longchamp's death. They ran northeast through the forest, crossed the moor to the Ridgeway, and then fled past the Red Oak to the Evil Hold. Two knights rode out of the Evil Hold the next morning, traveling east through the Barnisdale Wood. Ket the Trow left them on the road to Doncaster.

Ket the Trow then traveled to Outwoods, where he met Robert's steward, Scadlock, before going into the village. In the alehouse he heard that several villagers had been beaten that day and were making plans to overthrow Sir Guy of Gisborne. Robert knew that there was trouble ahead. He said goodbye to Marian, Sir Richard, and Lady Alice and walked to Outwoods.

As Robert came out of the woods a feeling of unease came over him. It was too quiet. No children were playing in the street, and no men were working in the fields. As he walked toward his house, a woman appeared in a doorway to signal him away. When he neared the house, he hid behind a tree near a man-at-arms who was watching something that amused him. Robert sneaked up behind the man and knocked him out.

The man had been watching another man-at-arms with a vicious whip with knotted ends standing in front of Scadlock and three villagers tied to posts surrounded by a group of jeering guards. A short distance away stood the guards' master, the vile Sir Hubert of Lynn, who commanded that each man should be given a hundred lashes before being put to death. As Robert watched, the flogging began. He sank to his knees and removed six arrows from his belt and laid them on the ground in front of him. Then he prayed that his shafts would be well guided.

Robert's first arrow killed Sir Hubert of Lynn. The second arrow was on its way before the first arrow struck. In rapid succession, Robert shot five of his six arrows, each of which found its target. Seeing five men die so quickly, the rest of Sir Hubert's men fled. Robert cut down Scadlock and the other villagers and took them into his house to dress their wounds.

Scadlock explained that the previous day Robert had been declared an outlaw from the steps of the cross at Pontefact. That morning Sir Hubert of Lynn had come to take possession of the house and lands for the abbot of St. Mary's Abbey. Scadlock and the three villagers that had been visiting Outwoods could do nothing to stop them. Robert asked the villagers whether they wanted to join him as outlaws living in the forest.

They heard people approaching the house, and Robert went out and greeted thirty more men from the village. They had come to offer their services and pledge their allegiance to Robert of Locksley, whom they had always known to be fair. The eldest among them, a man called Will the Bowman, told Robert that they would all follow him if he would agree to lead them.

Robert reminded them that if they went with him, their work-load would fall on the shoulders of their wives and children. A few were discouraged by these words and went quietly back to the village. Many others had suffered more than they could bear; they were determined to endure it no longer. They debated the merits of living as outlaws in the woods or remaining to suffer at the hands of Sir Guy of Gisborne, who would become their master the next day. The remaining fourteen villagers decided that they would be better off leading the lives of outlaws in the greenwood rather than putting up with degradation and suffering at the hands of Sir Guy of Gisborne.

Robert looked around and asked why Will Scarlet was not among them. He was told that Will had been caught killing a deer in the forest and would soon be taken from his cell to the courts of Doncaster, where his right hand would be cut off for his crime. This news removed all doubts from Robert's mind; he immediately agreed to lead the men. Will the Bowman turned to the others and made them all swear allegiance to Robert of Locksley, who told them that their first task was the release of Will Scarlet.

Robert told them that from that day until they again became free men, he would no longer be known as Robert of Locksley; instead, he would be called Robin Hood. He had always been known as Robin to those who knew and trusted him, and Hood because, until they once again walked as free men without a price on their heads, he would hide as if under a hooded tunic.

Robin Hood and his men stole away into the night through Fangthief Wood until they came to the village of Birkencar and the manor house of Sir Guy of Gisborne. The manor was dark as Robin led his small force up to the walls and took a few of them down to the underground cell where Will Scarlet was being held. Robin could make out Will's huddled form behind the stout door. Robin hacked the door open, and Scadlock and two other men pulled out the prisoner, who was badly injured. They laid him on the grass and tended his wounds.

Robin could see some of his men stacking great bundles of dried wood against the walls of the manor house. They set fire to the wood intending to burn Sir Guy of Gisborne alive. Robin reminded them that there were women in the house, who should be allowed to leave. One of the men raked the burning wood from the front door to permit the screaming women to escape. When the women were free, the man started to reposition the burning wood when he was fatally struck in the throat with a spear.

A cry was heard from the rear of the manor, which sent Robin and Will the Bowman running to see what the commotion was. When they reached the back of the house, they saw a storehouse with its doors wide open and found their comrades frightened almost out of their wits. They said that a Spectre Beast had burst from the storehouse and run up the hill. Will the Bowman chased after it. Robin knew that Sir Guy had given them the slip.

The housekeeper told Robin that two days earlier, Sir Guy had flayed a brown mare and had hung the skin in the storehouse to dry. Sir Guy had wrapped himself in the hide to make his escape.

With Sir Guy of Gisborne out of reach, probably rousing his comrades against Robin and his men, Robin led his weary, half-angry, half-happy group of peasants into the forest. There they would take sanctuary until the evil infecting the land could be overcome and once more they could walk free among their fellow men.

Robin Hood led his men deep into the heart of Sherwood Forest. Their camp was located at Stane Lea, or Stanley, where a small rivulet provided them with pure water. From this base, they began their to earn their reputation of taking from the rich and giving to the poor.

Moral: At times, we do not control our destiny; it controls us. Giving to the poor is a commendable virtue; however, taking from the rich is not.

Based on: Mike Dixon-Kennedy, "Legends of Robin Hood and His Merry Men," *The Robin Hood Handbook*

The Selection of Noah

The children of Adam and Eve had many children. When these grew up, they also had children, who, in turn, had children of their own. After a while, that part of the earth where Adam's sons lived became populated. As time passed, more and more of these people became wicked, and fewer and fewer of them grew up to be good men and women. All the people lived near one another; few moved to other lands. Eventually even the children of good men and women learned to be bad like the people around them.

God looked down on the world that he had made and saw how wicked the people in it had become. He decided to take away all men and women from the earth because they were evil. However, even in those bad times, God saw one good man. His name was Noah. Noah tried to do right in the sight of God. He walked with God and talked with Him.

God said to Noah, "The time has come when all men and women on the earth are to be destroyed. Everyone must die, because they are all wicked. But you and your family shall be saved, because you alone are trying to do right."

Then God told Noah how he might save his life and the lives of his family. He was to build a very large boat, as large as the largest ships ever built. It must be very long, very wide, and very deep— like a three-story house with a roof over it. Such a ship was called an "ark." God told Noah to build this ark and to have it ready for the time when it would be needed.

God told Noah, "I am going to bring a great flood of water upon the earth to cover all the land and to drown all the people in the world. Since the animals will be drowned with the people, you must make the ark large enough to hold a pair of each kind of animal, and more of certain animals needed by men, such as cattle, sheep, goats, and oxen, so that there will be animals as well as men to live upon the earth after the flood has subsided. You must take in the ark food for yourself and your family and for all the animals, enough food to last a year, while the flood shall stay on the earth."

Noah did what God had asked him to do. Noah and his sons worked on the ark for many years. It must have seemed strange to the people who lived around Noah to see this great ark being built where there was no water for it to float upon. At last the ark was finished. It looked like a great house with a door on one side and an opening in the roof to let in the light and air.

Then God said to Noah, "Come into the ark, you and you wife and your three sons and their wives because the floodwaters will come very soon. Take with you animals of all kinds, and birds, and things that creep. Take seven pairs of those that will be needed by men and one pair of all the rest, so that all kinds of animals may be kept alive upon the earth."

Noah and his wife and his three sons, Shem, Ham, and Japheth, and their wives went into the ark. God brought the animals, the birds, and the creeping things to the door of the vessel. Noah and his sons took them into the ark, put them in their pens, and brought food aboard for the people and the animals. Then the door of the ark was closed, so that no more people or animals could come aboard.

Within a few days it began to rain as it had never rained before. It seemed as though the heavens had opened up to pour great floods upon the earth. The streams filled and the rivers rose higher and higher until the ark began to float upon the water. People left their homes and ran to the hilltops, but soon the hills were covered. All the people on them drowned. Some people climbed to the tops of the highest mountains, but the water again rose higher and higher, until even the mountains were covered, and those people also drowned in the great sea that now covered all the earth where men had lived.

All the animals, the tame animals—cattle, sheep, goats and oxen, and the wild animals—lions, tigers, and all the rest, were drowned also. Even the birds drowned, because their nests in the trees were swept away, and there was no place for them to land. For forty days and forty nights the rain continued, until there was no breath of life remaining outside the ark. The rain stopped after forty days, but the water stayed on the earth for more than six months. The ark and all that were in it floated over the great sea that covered the land.

Then God sent a wind to blow over the waters and dry them up. By degrees, the level of the water went down. After waiting a few months, Noah released a raven through the opening in the roof of the ark. The raven, with its strong wings, flew around and around and found a place to land, so it did not return to the ark. Noah waited a while longer and then sent out a dove. The dove couldn't find a place to land, so it returned to the ark. Noah waited another week and released the dove again. This time the dove returned home to the ark with a fresh leaf from an olive tree in its beak.

Noah now knew that the water had gone down enough to let the trees grow once more. He waited another week before sending out the dove again. This time the dove flew away and did not return. Noah knew that the earth was becoming dry again. God said to Noah, "Come out of the ark, with your wife and your sons and their wives and all the living things that are with you."

Noah opened the door of the ark and came out with his family, who once more stood on solid ground. All the animals, birds, and creeping things left the ark also and began to bring life back to the earth. The first thing that Noah did when he left the ark was to give thanks to God for saving his family when the rest of the people on earth had been destroyed. He built an altar, laid upon it an offering to the Lord, gave himself and his family to God, and promised to do God's will.

God was pleased with Noah's offering, and He said, "I will not again destroy the earth on account of men, no matter how bad they may be. From this time on, no flood shall again cover the earth. The seasons of spring, summer, fall, and winter shall remain without change. I give to you the earth. You shall be the rulers of the earth and of every living thing on it."

Then God created a rainbow to appear in the sky, and he told Noah and his sons that whenever they or the people who came after them saw a rainbow, they should remember that God placed it in the sky as a sign of the promise that he would always remember the earth and the people upon it and would never again send a flood to destroy them. When we see a rainbow, we should remember that it is the sign of God's promise to the world.

* * *

"In the central part of Armenia stands an exceeding large and high mountain [Mt. Ararat], upon which, it is said, the Ark of Noah rested, and for this reason it is termed the 'Mountain of the Ark.'"

Marco Polo, AD 1300

"There simply could not have been an Ark as described in the Bible. It would have had to accommodate 3,858,920 animals. If the dimensions of the craft as laid out in Genesis are accepted, that is a snug one-quarter cubic foot per beast."

Robert Moore, *Maclean's* magazine

"If God was able to create the entire world, and the sun, moon, stars and planets, plus entire galaxies in space beyond our imagination, could God not feed animals and people in a large boat for 150 days?"

Mark Peterson, *Noah and the Flood*

Moral: If we are good, it will be recognized.

Based on: Jesse Lyman Hurlbut, "The Great Ship That Saved Eight People," *Hurlbut's Story of the Bible for the Young and Old* and *The Holy Bible*

The Prince Who Would Seek Immortality

Centuries ago, a city in the middle of a large kingdom had a castle and a king. The king thought his son was wiser and more clever than any other son. He carefully chose tutors and governors for the young man and encouraged him to travel to learn the ways of other people.

When the prince had been home a year after his travels, his father thought it was time for him to learn how to rule the kingdom that would soon be his. During his long absence, the prince's character seemed to have changed. From being a light-hearted, happy boy, he had become a thoughtful, gloomy young man. The king knew of no reason for the change and was perplexed by it. Finally, he decided that his son must be in love.

The prince never talked about his feelings; in fact, he didn't talk much at all. One evening after dinner, the king took his son into a room with many pictures of beautiful maidens. He suggested that his son marry and offered to send an emissary to the father of any one of the young women to ask for her hand in marriage.

The prince told his father that it wasn't love or desire for marriage that made him gloomy, but the thought that all men, even kings, must die. The prince said that he could never be happy again until he found a kingdom where death was unknown. He was determined to discover the Land of Immortality.

The king was dismayed; things were worse than he thought. He tried to reason with his son, reminding the young man that he had been waiting for the prince to return from his travels and assume the cares of the kingdom. The prince would not listen. The next morning he strapped on his sword and set forth on his journey.

The prince had traveled for many days when close to the road he came upon a huge tree with an eagle sitting on its topmost bough, shaking the branches violently. This was so strange and unlike an eagle that the surprised prince stood and watched. The eagle saw him and flew down. The moment its feet touched the ground, the eagle turned into a king.

The eagle king asked the prince why he looked so surprised. The young man answered that he wondered why the eagle had been shaking the branches so fiercely. The eagle king explained that he was condemned to do it because neither he nor any of his relatives could die until he had uprooted that great tree. It was evening and the eagle king did not need to work any more that day. He invited the prince to come home with him as his guest for the night.

Tired and hungry, the prince gratefully accepted the eagle king's invitation. The king's beautiful daughter served dinner to them. While they were eating, the king asked about the purpose of the prince's travels. The prince told them everything, including the fact that he wouldn't turn back until he had discovered the Land of Immortality.

The king told the prince that he had found it. He said that death had no power over either him or his relatives until he had uprooted the tree, which the king estimated would take six hundred years. He added that after all six hundred years is virtually an eternity. The king offered his daughter in marriage if the prince would stay with them.

The prince turned down the king's offer, because after six hundred years, they would have to die and would then be no better off. The prince told the king that he must continue his travels until he found a country where there was no death at all. The princess tried to persuade him to stay, but without success. Seeing that he was determined to leave, the princess gave him a small box containing her picture. She told him that if he took out this box on his travels and looked at her picture, he would be borne along swiftly either on the earth or in the air. He thanked her and said goodbye to the king and his daughter.

The prince was very thankful to the princess for her gift. He used it on many occasions. One evening it carried him to the top of a high mountain, where he saw a man with a bald head digging up spadefuls of earth and throwing them in a basket. The man then took the full basket away and returned with an empty one, which he filled. The prince asked the bald-headed man why he was filling the baskets.

The man told the prince that he was condemned to do it, for neither he nor any of his family could die until he had dug away the entire mountain and made it level with the plain. It was almost dark. The man quit digging and was transformed into a stately bald-headed king. The king invited the prince to his home, where his daughter had dinner waiting for them. The prince accepted and was greeted at the door by the princess, who was even more beautiful than the other princess. The king asked the prince about the purpose of his travels and was told about the quest for the Land of Immortality.

The king told the prince that he had found it, since neither he nor his family could die until he had leveled the great mountain, which was going to take another eight hundred years. The king asked the prince to stay with them and to marry his daughter. He said that eight hundred years was surely long enough to live. The prince told him that he would rather seek the land where there was no death at all.

The next morning the prince left on his travels despite the pleading of the princess. She gave him a gold ring as a remembrance. The ring was even more useful than the box because when one wished to be someplace, he or she was transported there directly without the trouble of flying through the air. The prince thanked the princess heartily.

The prince walked some distance and decided to try the ring. He closed his eyes and wished to be at the end of the world. When he opened his eyes he was standing in a street full of marble palaces. The men who passed him were tall and strong, and their clothes were stylish. He stopped some of them and asked in all of the languages that he knew what the name of the city was. No one answered, and he wondered what he would do if nobody could understand him.

Suddenly the prince saw a man dressed in the fashion of his own native country. He inquired in his tongue what city he was in. The man told the prince that he was in the capital of the Blue Kingdom and that the king had died and his daughter was now the ruler. The prince asked the man to take him to the young queen's palace, which was a splendid edifice supported by slender pillars of soft green marble. The queen was occupied by listening to the problems of her people.

When the prince approached her, she could see that he was no ordinary man. She asked her chamberlain to dismiss the rest of her petitioners for the day and invited the prince to accompany her into the palace. She had been taught his language as a child; they had no difficulty in communicating. The prince told the queen about his search for the Land of Immortality. When he had finished speaking, the queen led him to the door of another room, the floor of which was made entirely of needles stuck so close together that there was no room for another needle.

The queen explained to the prince that neither she nor any of her family could die until she had worn out all these needles in sewing. She estimated that it would take a thousand years. She invited him to stay with her at the palace and share her throne. She said that a thousand years is long enough to live. The prince observed that at the end of that time he would still have to die. He told her that he would continue to seek the land where there is no death. She tried unsuccessfully to persuade him to stay. Finally, she gave him a small golden rod as a remembrance of her. It had the power to become anything he wished it to be when he was in need. He thanked her and went on his way.

Just outside the city, the prince came to a broad river that no man could pass, for it was the river that flowed around the end of the world. He walked up the bank of the river and could see a beautiful city floating in the air over his head. He wanted to go there, but neither a bridge nor a road led to it. He thought that this was the land he was seeking. He tried the golden rod that the queen had given him. He flung it to the ground, wishing for a bridge. A golden ladder appeared, leading to the city in the clouds.

As the prince entered the golden gates to the city, a terrible beast sprung at him. He ordered his sword out of its scabbard. It cut off some of the monster's heads, but others grew again to replace them. The prince, pale with terror, put his sword back in its sheath and called for help. The queen of the city heard his plea and summoned her servants to rescue the stranger and bring him to her. The queen realized that he was no ordinary man and welcomed him to the city. She asked what brought him there, and the prince explained about his search for the Land of Immortality. The queen told the prince that he had found it. She said that she was the queen over life and over death, and that there he could dwell among the immortals.

A thousand years passed after the prince entered the city. Time had gone by so fast that it seemed like no more than six months. The prince had not been unhappy for one instant during the thousand years, until one night he dreamed of his father and mother. The longing for home came upon him in a rush, and in the morning he told the Queen of Immortals that he must go and see his father and mother one more time. The queen stared at him with amazement and reminded him that it had been more that nine hundred years since his parents had died. Not even their dust would remain. The prince said that he must go anyway.

The queen realized that she could not talk the prince out of his journey. She offered to help him prepare for his venture. She unlocked her great treasure chest and took out two beautiful flasks, one of gold and the other silver, which she hung around his neck. She showed him a trapdoor in a corner of the room and instructed him to fill the silver flask with the water below the trapdoor. She told him that the water was enchanted, and that whoever he sprinkled with the water would die at once, even if he had lived a thousand years. The queen instructed the prince to fill the golden flask from a well in another corner of the room, adding that it sprung from the rock of eternity. She told him that sprinkling a few drops on a body would cause it to come to life again, even if it had been dead for a thousand years.

The prince thanked the queen for her gifts and departed. He soon arrived in the city where he had stopped before arriving in the

Land of Immortality. The city had changed dramatically, and he had difficulty finding his way to the palace. When he found the palace, it was quiet. He went to the queen's chamber and found her apparently asleep. After he could not awaken her, he went to the room where the needles were kept and found it empty. The queen had used the last needle and had broken the spell and died.

The prince pulled out the golden flask and sprinkled some drops over the queen. She opened her eyes and thanked him for awakening her. He told her that she would have slept for an eternity if he had not wakened her. She thanked him and offered to repay him if she got the chance.

The prince left to travel to the land of the bald-headed king. As he approached the place where he had seen the king, he saw that the entire mountain had been dug away. The king was lying dead on the ground with his spade and bucket beside him. As soon as the water from the golden flask touched him, he awoke and got to his feet. He told the prince he was glad to see him, and that he must have slept a long while. The prince replied that the king would have slept forever if he hadn't wakened him. The king remembered the mountain and the spell and vowed to repay the favor if he got the opportunity.

Further down the road to his home, the prince found the great tree torn up by its roots and the king of eagles dead on the ground with his wings spread. A few drops of water brought the king around, and he expressed his thanks for being awakened. When the king commented on how long he had slept, the prince said that the king would have slept for an eternity if he hadn't come along. The king remembered the tree and realized that he had been dead. He promised to repay the prince if he had the chance.

At last the prince reached the capital of his father's kingdom. Instead of finding the royal palace, he found a great sulphur lake with blue flames leaping into the air. He wondered how he could find his father and mother if they were lying at the bottom of that horrible lake. He turned away in despair, hardly knowing where he was going.

A voice behind the prince cried out, "Stop! I've caught you at last." Beside him stood the white-bearded figure of Death. Swiftly the prince drew the ring from his finger, and the king of eagles, the bald-headed king, and the sewing queen came to his rescue. They seized Death and held him tight until the prince had time to get back to the Land of Immortality. Unfortunately, they didn't realize how fast Death could fly. The prince had only one foot across the border when he felt his other foot being grabbed by Death.

The Queen of Immortals was watching from her window and called out to Death that he had no jurisdiction within her kingdom. Death told her that one foot was in his kingdom and that the prince belonged to him. The queen observed that half was in her kingdom and asked what could Death would do with half a man. The queen asked Death to step into the Land of Immortality while they decided by wager to whom the prince belonged. The queen offered to throw the prince up into the sky to the back of the morning star. She told Death that if the prince fell back down into the city, he was hers; however, if he fell outside the walls, he belonged to Death. Death agreed to the terms

The event took place in the middle of the city square. The queen placed her foot under the prince's foot and flung him high into the sky. He went so high that he was out of sight. The queen hoped that she had thrown him up straight or he would be lost forever. Finally they could see a speck falling to earth. As the prince neared the city, a light wind sprang up, causing him to drift toward the castle wall. As he landed, the queen sprang forward, seized him in her arms, and flung him into the castle. She commanded her servants to cast Death out of the city, which they did with such hard blows that he never appeared again in the Land of Immortality.

Moral: Be careful what you wish for; you might get it.

Based on: Andrew Lang, "The Prince Who Would Seek
    Immortality," *The Crimson Fairy Book*

The Blind Men and the Elephant
There once were six blind men who stood by the side of the road every day and begged from people who passed. They had heard of elephants but had never seen one. After all, how could they? All three men had been blind since birth.

One morning an elephant was driven down the road where the men begged. When they were told that the beast was in front of them, they asked the driver to stop so that they could learn more about the animal. They hoped that by touching the elephant they could find out what kind of animal it was.

The first blind man put his hand on the elephant's side and exclaimed that he knew all about the beast. An elephant was just like a wall. The second blind man felt only the elephant's tusk and told the first man that he was mistaken; the elephant was round, smooth, and sharp; in fact, the elephant was more like a spear than anything else.

The third blind man approached the elephant and took the squirming trunk in his hands. He told the first two blind men that they were wrong; the elephant was like a snake. The fourth blind man reached out and grabbed one of the elephant's legs. He told the first three men that they really were blind; the elephant was round and tall like a tree.

The fifth blind man was very tall; when he reached out, he took hold of the elephant's ear. He said that the first four men didn't know what they were talking about; an elephant was like a huge fan. The sixth blind man had trouble finding the elephant and when he did, he found the swinging tail. He told the other five men that an elephant wasn't like a wall, a spear, a snake, a tree, or a fan; an elephant was exactly like a rope.

These six men each had a strong opinion and argued long and loudly. Although each was partly right, all of them were also partly wrong. Frequently participants in an argument base their opinions on incomplete information and are unwilling to accept the insights of others.

Moral: Respect the opinions of others and recognize that they may be approaching the subject from a different, but not necessarily an inferior, point of view.

Based on: James Baldwin, "The Blind Men and the Elephant," *Favorite Tales of Long Ago*
Ralph L. Woods, "The Blind Men and the Elephant," *A Treasury of the Familiar*

The Legend of Pandora's Box

Thousands of years ago there lived a child named Epimetheus who had neither a father nor a mother. Another fatherless and motherless child like himself was sent from a far away country to live with him, so that he wouldn't be lonely. The name of this playfellow and helpmate was Pandora.

The first thing that Pandora noticed when she entered the cottage where Epimetheus lived was a great box. She asked what was in the box. Epimetheus answered that it was a secret and not to ask questions about it. He told her that the box had been left there to be kept safely, and that he didn't know what was in it. When she asked who had given it to him and where it had come from, Epimetheus told her that those were secrets too. These answers provoked Pandora. She wished that the great box were out of the way. Epimetheus told her to think no more about it and asked her to come outside and play with the other children.

Epimetheus and Pandora had a very pleasant life with neither work nor studying to do. They participated in sports activities and dances and never quarreled. Children of the time never sulked and knew nothing of troubles. The greatest concern was probably Pandora's annoyance at not being able to discover the secret of the box. This irritation grew more and more substantial every day until, before long, the cottage of Epimetheus and Pandora was loaded with tension. Pandora continued to ask where the box had come from, and what could be in it.

Epimetheus grew very tired of the subject and asked Pandora to talk of something else. He suggested that they go and pick some figs and grapes for their supper. When Pandora expressed no interest in that, he suggested that they go out and play with their playmates. She wasn't interested in that either. The only thing that she could think about was the box. She insisted that he tell her what was inside it, which he couldn't do because he didn't know. She suggested that they open it and find out for themselves.

Epimetheus was horrified by her suggestion. He wouldn't think of looking into a box that had been entrusted to his care on the condition that he would never open it. Pandora asked how it came to be there, and Epimetheus told her that it had been left at the door by a smiling, intelligent-looking person just before Pandora had arrived. The deliverer wore an odd cloak and a cap made partly out of feathers. Pandora inquired about the man's staff and Epimetheus told her that it had two lifelike serpents curling around the stick.

Pandora said that she knew the deliverer; nobody else had a staff like that. It was Quicksilver, the man who had brought her there. Pandora thought that, no doubt, he intended the box for her, probably pretty dresses for her to wear or toys for her to play with. Epimetheus said that it was possible, but until Quicksilver returned and approved of opening the box, neither of them had the right to open it.

Pandora thought about what a dull boy Epimetheus was and wished that he were more enterprising. For the first time since Pandora had arrived, Epimetheus went out by himself to pick figs and grapes and to play with their friends. He was really tired of Pandora's harping about the box.

After Epimetheus had gone, Pandora stood gazing at the box. It really was an attractive piece of furniture, an ornament in any room in which it was placed. It was made of beautiful dark, rich wood, which was so highly polished that Pandora could see her reflection in it. The edges and corners had been carved with skill and around the margin were figures of graceful men and women and pretty children reclining amid a profusion of flowers and foliage. These objects were so exquisitely represented and were brought together in such harmony that flowers, foliage, and human beings seemed to combine in a wreath of mingled beauty.

Occasionally, Pandora could see, peeping out from behind the carved foliage, a face not so lovely or something disagreeable that stole the beauty from all the rest. Looking closely and touching it with her fingers, she could discover nothing of the kind. It was as though a beautiful face had been made to look ugly when catching a sideways glimpse of it.

The most beautiful face was done in high relief in the center of the lid. Pandora looked at this face many times and imagined that the mouth could smile if it liked or be sad when it chose, the same as any living mouth. Its features wore a very lively and rather mischievous expression, which looked as though it could burst out of the carved lips and utter words.

The box was fastened not by a lock but by an intricate knot of gold cord, which appeared to have no beginning and no end. The knot was so cunningly twisted that it defied the most skillful fingers to disentangle it. Because of its very difficulty, Pandora was even more challenged to examine the knot to see how it was made. She thought that she could see how it was tied and was tempted to untie it and then tie it up again. If Pandora had work to do around the cottage, her mind might have been diverted from the box, but light sweeping and dusting and gathering of flowers were not enough to divert her.

Pandora tried to lift the box, but it was too heavy; however, she was able to lift it a few inches off the floor. She let it fall with a loud thump and thought that she heard something stir within the box. There seemed to be a kind of stifled murmur from within. She took the knot in her fingers and was determined to find the ends of the gold cord. While listening to the voices of children playing outside, she tried to untie the knot. The face in relief in the cover of the box seemed to be smiling at her. She was tempted to run away.

Just then, she twisted the knot and the gold cord untwined itself and left the box without a fastening. She tried twice to retie the knot, but it was beyond her skill. She considered leaving the box unopened until Epimetheus returned. However, when he saw the knot untied, he would know that she had done it. She wondered how she could convince him that she had not looked into it. She decided that if she were going to be suspected of looking into the box, she might as well do it. Pandora decided to take one little peek into the box. What harm would there possibly be in one peek?

Epimetheus played with his friends, but he wasn't used to playing outside without Pandora, and he missed her. Nothing seemed right with his other playmates. He decided to go in and play with Pandora and to take her a wreath of flowers made of roses, lilies, and orange blossoms.

A great black cloud had been growing in the sky and had began to block the sun just as he entered the doorway to the cottage. He intended to enter softly to surprise Pandora with the flowers but there was no need to be quiet since she was totally occupied with the box. The hands of the naughty girl were on the lid of the box when Epimetheus entered the cottage.

Epimetheus could have cried out for Pandora to stop, but he didn't. He was curious as well about the contents of the box and if anything valuable was in it, he intended to have half. He was nearly as much at fault as she.

As Pandora raised the lid, the cottage grew dark and dismal. The black cloud covered the sun, and thunder could be heard in the distance. Pandora lifted the lid all the way and looked inside. A sudden swarm of winged creatures brushed past her. She heard Epimetheus cry out in pain. He told her that he had been stung and asked why she had opened the box.

Pandora could hear a loud buzzing of ugly little shapes with bats' wings, looking threatening and armed with long stingers in their tails. One of these had stung Epimetheus, and another had settled on Pandora's forehead. Epimetheus brushed it away before it could sting her.

The ugly things that had escaped from the box were the whole family of earthly troubles, including evil Passions, many species of Cares, over a hundred and fifty Sorrows, Diseases in miserable and painful shapes, and many kinds of Naughtiness. In a time of little or no trouble, everything that has since afflicted the souls and bodies of mankind had been shut up in the box and given to Epimetheus and Pandora to be kept safely, so the happy children of the world might never be harmed by them.

If Epimetheus and Pandora had been faithful to their trust, all would have been well. No grown person would ever have been sad, nor any child have had cause to shed a single tear, from then until the present moment.

By Pandora's opening the box and by Epimetheus's not preventing her from doing it, these Troubles have gained a foothold among us and do not seem likely to go away. It was not possible for the two children to keep the ugly swarm captive in their little cottage. In fact, the first thing they did was to fling open the doors and windows to get rid of them. The winged Troubles flew everywhere and pestered and tormented people. Even the flowers and blossoms began to droop.

Pandora and Epimetheus stayed in their cottage. Both had been stung and were in pain, the first pain they had ever experienced. They were in bad humor, both with themselves and with each other. Epimetheus sulked, and Pandora cried. Then they heard a gentle tap on the inside of the lid of the box and wondered what it could be. It sounded like the tiny knuckles of a fairy's hand knocking lightly on the inside of the box. They called out, inquiring who was inside the box and were told to lift the lid and see.

Pandora refused to lift the lid. She had gotten into too much trouble the last time that she did. Epimetheus declined to lift it also. The sweet voice said that she was not like those naughty creatures with stings in their tails and if they could see her, they would let her out. Pandora asked Epimetheus if she should lift the lid and he said that so much mischief had been done already, they might as well take a chance on a little more. The owner of the voice asked again to be let out, and the children lifted the lid together.

A sunny, smiling little personage flew out of the box and hovered about the room, casting light wherever she went. The winged fairy-like stranger spread cheerfulness around the cottage. She flew to Epimetheus and put a finger on his forehead where he had been stung, and immediately the pain was relieved. She did the same for Pandora with a kiss on the forehead.

Epimetheus and Pandora asked the beautiful creature who she was, and she told them that she was called Hope. She explained that because she was such a cheery little body, she had been packed into the box to make amends to the human race for the swarm of ugly Troubles destined to be let loose among them. Hope told them not to fear, that they would do well in spite of them. The children saw that Hope's wings were the colors of the rainbow. She explained that, glad as her nature was, she was made partly of tears and partly of smiles.

Pandora asked Hope if she would stay with them. She said that she would stay as long as she was needed. Hope said that she would be with them as long as they lived; she would never desert them. Hope admitted that there would be times when they would think that she had vanished but that, again and again, they would see the glimmer of her wings on the ceiling of their cottage.

Hope told them that something very good and beautiful would be given to them hereafter. They asked what it was and were told that they should not despair if it never happened while they lived upon this earth. Hope asked them to trust in her promise because it was true. Epimetheus and Pandora told Hope that they trusted her, and so has everyone who has lived trusted Hope.

Moral: Curiosity should be controlled. No matter how bad
     life gets, never give up hope that it will get better.

Based on: Nathaniel Hawthorne, "The Paradise of Children,"
     The Wonder Book

Chapter 2

NOTABLE / LOYAL

When young we are faithful to individuals; when older we grow more loyal to situations and to types.

Cyril Connolly, *The Unquiet Grave*

Lost on Dress Parade

Mr. Towers Chandler was pressing his evening suit in his hall bed-room. He was pushing the iron vigorously back and forth to make the desirable crease that would be seen later extending in straight lines from Mr. Chandler's patent leather shoes to the edge of his low-cut vest. Our next view of his genteel poverty comes as he descends the stairs of his lodging house immaculately and correct-ly dressed: calm, assured, handsome—in appearance the typical New York clubman setting out, slightly bored, to inaugurate the pleasures of the evening.

Chandler's weekly salary was small. He was twenty-two years old and employed in the office of an architect. He considered archi-tecture truly an art; he honestly believed, although he would not have dared to admit it, that the Flatiron building in Manhattan was inferior in design to the great cathedral in Milan.

Chandler set aside a small amount from each week's earnings to pay for an occasional gentleman's evening out. He arrayed him-self in the regalia of millionaires and presidents; he went where life was brightest and showiest and dined in luxury. With his small sav-ings, he could, for a few hours, play the wealthy idler to perfection. A small sum was enough for a good meal, a bottle of wine with a respectable label, tips, a smoke, cab fare, and the usual extras.

This one delectable evening culled from seventy dull ones was to Chandler a source of bliss. To the young woman comes but one debut into society; it stands alone sweet in her memory when her hair has whitened. Every ten weeks brought to Chandler a joy as keen, as thrilling, as new as the first had been. To sit among people of refined taste under palm trees in the swirl of concealed music, to look upon the frequenters of such a paradise and be looked upon by them—what is a girl's first dance compared with this?

Chandler moved up Broadway with the evening dress parade. This evening he was an exhibit as well as a gazer. For the next sixty-nine evenings he would be dining in worsted at dubious lunch counters or on sandwiches and beer in his bedroom. He was will-ing to do that, because he considered himself a true son of the great city of razzle-dazzle. To him, one evening in the limelight made up for the many dark ones.

Chandler extended his walk until the Forties began to intersect Broadway. The evening was still young, and when one is a member of the world of fashionable society only one day in seventy, one loves to prolong the pleasure. Eyes bright, sinister, curious, admiring, provocative, and alluring were cast upon him, for his garb and air proclaimed him a devotee of pleasure.

Chandler stopped at the corner where he had to decide whether to turn back toward the showy and fashionable restaurant where he usually dined on the evenings of his special luxury. Just then a girl skidded around the corner, slipped on an icy patch of snow, and fell to the sidewalk. Chandler helped her to her feet and was very solicitous. The girl hobbled to the wall of the nearby building, leaned against it, and thanked him demurely.

The girl told Chandler that she had twisted her ankle when she fell and thought that she might have sprained it. He asked if she was in pain, and she said only when she put weight on her ankle. Chandler asked if he could be of any further service and offered to call a cab for her. She thanked him and told him that he wouldn't have to trouble himself any further. She admitted that it had been awkward of her, particularly since she was wearing shoes with practical heels.

Chandler looked at the girl and found that she drew his interest. She was pretty in a refined way; her eyes were merry and kind. She was inexpensively clothed in a plain black dress such as shop girls wear. Her glossy dark-brown hair showed its coils beneath an inexpensive hat of black straw whose only ornament was a velvet ribbon and bow. She could have posed as a model for the self-respecting working girl of the best type.

A sudden idea came into Chandler's head. He should ask this girl to dine with him. His splendid but solitary feasts had lacked something. His brief time of elegant luxury would be doubly enjoyable if he could add a lady's society to it. This girl was a lady, he was sure—her manner and speech indicated that. Despite her plain attire, he felt that he would like to dine with her.

These thoughts passed through the young architect's mind, and he decided to ask her. It was a breach of etiquette, of course, but sometimes working girls waived formalities in matters of this kind. Usually they were shrewd judges of men. They valued their own judgment more than useless conventions. The money that he had set aside for this evening's entertainment would enable them to dine very well. No doubt the dinner would be a wonderful experience thrown into the dull routine of the girl's life. Her lively appreciation would add to his own pleasure.

Chandler told her that he thought that her ankle needed a longer rest than she supposed. He told her that there was a way she could give it more rest and at the same time do him a favor. He said that he was on his way to a lonely dinner when she came tumbling around the corner. He asked her to come with him so they could have an enjoyable dinner and a pleasant talk together, and by that time her rested ankle would carry her home very nicely.

The girl looked quickly up into Chandler's pleasant countenance. Her eyes twinkled once very briefly, and then she smiled ingenuously and said, "But we don't know each other—it wouldn't be right, would it?" The young man said that there was nothing wrong with it. "I'll introduce myself—permit me—Mr. Towers Chandler. After our dinner, which I will try to make as pleasant as possible, I will bid you good evening or take you safely to your door, whichever you prefer."

"But, dear me!" said the girl, with a glance at Chandler's faultless attire. "In this old dress and hat."

"Never mind that," said Chandler, cheerfully. "I'm sure you look more charming in them than anyone we shall see in the most elaborate dinner dress."

She admitted that her ankle still hurt as she tried a limping step. "I think I will accept your invitation, Mr. Chandler. You may call me—Miss Marian."

"Come then, Miss Marian," said the architect with perfect courtesy, "You will not have far to walk. A very respectable restaurant is located in the next block. You will have to lean on my arm and walk slowly. It is lonely dining by one's self. I am just a little bit glad that you slipped on the ice."

When they were seated at a well-appointed table with a promising waiter hovering in attendance, Chandler began to experience the real joy that his regular outing always brought to him. The tables were filled with prosperous-looking diners, a good orchestra was playing softly enough to permit pleasant conversation, and the cuisine and service were beyond criticism.

Chandler's companion, even in her inexpensive hat and dress, held herself with an air that added distinction to the natural beauty of her face and figure. She looked at Chandler, with his animated but self-possessed manner and his kindly blue eyes, with something not far from admiration.

It was then that the Madness of Manhattan, the Bacillus of Brag, and the Plague of Pose seized upon Towers Chandler. He was on Broadway, surrounded by pomp and style, and there were eyes looking at him. On the stage of that comedy he had assumed to play the one-night part of a butterfly of fashion and an idler of means and taste. He was dressed for the part, and all of his good angels did not have the power to prevent him from acting it.

Chandler began to talk to Miss Marian about clubs, teas, golf, riding, cotillions, tours abroad, and he threw out hints of a yacht berthed at Larchmont. He saw that she was impressed by this talk so he inflated his pose by random insinuations of great wealth and mentioned with familiarity a few prominent names. It was Chandler's day, and he wrang from it the most that he could. Once or twice he saw the pure gold of this girl shine through the mist that his egotism had raised.

Miss Marian observed that the way of living that he had described sounded futile and purposeless. She asked him if he had any work to do in the world that might interest him more. Chandler exclaimed, "My dear Miss Marian—work! Think of making half a dozen calls in the afternoon and dressing every day for dinner. We do-nothings are the hardest workers in the land."

When dinner was concluded and the waiter generously tipped, they walked out to the corner where they had met. Miss Marian walked very well now; her limp was scarcely noticeable. She thanked him for a nice time, and said that she must start for home. She told him that she had enjoyed the dinner very much.

Chandler shook hands with her, smiling cordially, and said something about a game of bridge at his club. He watched her for a moment walking rapidly eastward and then took a cab home. In his chilly bedroom, Chandler laid away his evening clothes for a sixty-nine days' rest. He went about it thoughtfully.

Chandler thought, "That was a stunning girl. She's all right, too, even if she has to work. Perhaps if I'd told her the truth instead of all that razzle-dazzle we might—but, I had to live up to my clothes."

Miss Marian, after leaving her dinner companion, walked swiftly across town until she arrived at a sedate mansion on Fifth

Avenue. She entered hurriedly and went up to a room where an attractive young lady in an elaborate house dress looked anxiously out of the window.

Miss Marian's older sister exclaimed, "When will you quit frightening us this way? It has been two hours since you ran out in that old rag of a dress and Marie's hat. Mamma was so alarmed that she sent Louis in the car to find you. You are thoughtless." The older girl pressed a button and a maid entered the room. She said, "Marie, tell momma that Miss Marian has returned."

Miss Marian told her sister not to scold, and that she had only run down to Madam Theo's to tell her of a color change to the dress she was making for her. "My plain dress and Marie's hat were just what I needed. Everyone thought I was a shopgirl." Her sister told her that she was too late for dinner.

Miss Marion explained to her sister that she had slipped on the sidewalk, turned her ankle, and hobbled to a restaurant until it was better. She said that was why she took so long. The girls sat in the window seat, looking out at the lights and the stream of hurrying vehicles on the avenue.

Miss Marion observed that both of them would have to marry some day. "We have so much money that we will not be allowed to disappoint the public." Miss Marian asked her sister if she would like to know the type of man she could love. Her sister that she certainly would.

"I could love a man with kind blue eyes, who is respectful to poor girls, who is handsome and does not try to flirt. But I could love him only if he had an ambition, an object, some work to do in the world. I would not care how poor he was if I could help him build his way up. But, sister dear, the kind of man we always meet—the man who lives an idle life between society and his clubs—I could not love a man like that, even if his eyes were blue and he were ever so kind to poor girls whom he met in the street."

Moral: Be yourself. Representing yourself as someone else
       invites eventual discovery.

Based on: O. Henry, "Lost on Dress Parade," *The Four Million*

The Five Wise Words of the Guru

Once there lived a handsome young man named Ram Singh, who although he was popular was unhappy because his stepmother was a scold. She talked all day long until the youth was driven to distraction. He decided to go away to seek his fortune. He left the next morning with little money in his pocket and few clothes.

Before leaving the village, Ram Singh stopped to visit his teacher, a wise old guru who had taught him well. The old man received his pupil affectionately; however, he saw at once that the youth was troubled. He asked his pupil what the matter was and was told that he was determined to go out into the world to seek his fortune. The guru advised against it and told the youth that it was better to have half a loaf at home than a whole loaf in distant countries.

The old man could see that Ram Singh's mind was made up and could not be changed. He offered his pupil five pieces of advice. First—obey without question the orders of the person whose service you enter; second—never speak harshly or unkindly to anyone; third—never lie; fourth—never try to appear to be the equal to those above you in station; and fifth—wherever you go, if you meet those who who read or teach from the holy books, stay and listen, if but for a few minutes, that you may be strengthened spiritually. Ram Singh promised to obey the old man's advice and started out on his journey.

Eventually Ram Singh came to a great city. He had spent all of his money, so he looked for work. He saw a prosperous-looking merchant standing in front of a shop full of grain of all kinds and asked him for a job. The merchant told him that he knew of a place for him. The rajah's chief vizier had dismissed his manservant and needed a replacement. The merchant told him that he was just the sort of person that the vizier needed: young, tall, and handsome. Ram Singh thanked the merchant for his advice and obtained the position as the vizier's servant.

Several days later, the rajah of the palace started on a journey and the chief vizier accompanied him. With them was an army of servants, attendants, soldiers, muleteers, camel drivers, grain merchants, singers, and musicians along with elephants, camels, horses, mules, donkeys, goats, and carts and wagons of all kinds. It seemed more like a large town on the march than anything else.

The caravan traveled for several days until they entered a land that was like a sea of sand. They came to a village and were greeted by the headmen who hurried out to salute the rajah and to pay him their respects. The headmen explained with serious faces that although they were at the disposal of the rajah, they had did not have a well or spring to provide water for such a large army of men and beasts. The rajah told the host that he must get water somehow. That settled the matter as far as he was concerned.

The vizier questioned the oldest men in the place and asked them about sources of water. One wizened old man told the vizier that, within a mile of two of the village, was a well that a former king had made hundreds of years ago. It was said to be large and inexhaustible, covered by stonework with a flight of steps leading down to the water in the very bowels of the earth. No man ever went near it because it was haunted by evil spirits, and that no one who went down into the well was ever seen again.

The vizier stroked his beard, thought deeply, and turned to Ram Singh. He quoted a proverb that no man can be trusted until he had been tried. The vizier directed him to go and get the rajah and his people water from the well. Ram Singh remembered the first counsel of the guru: always obey without question the orders of the person whose service you enter.

Ram Singh left at once to prepare for his adventure. He fastened two great brass vessels to a mule and tied two lesser ones to his shoulders and set out with the old villager as his guide. Soon they came to a place where large trees towered above the barren country and cast shadows on the dome of an ancient building. His guide told him that this was the well and that because he was a tired old man who wanted to be home by sunset, he was going no further. Ram Singh bade him farewell and continued on with the mule.

Ram Singh tied up the mule near the trees, lifted the vessels from his shoulders, and descended a flight of stairs that led down into the darkness. The steps were broad slabs of alabaster that gleamed in the shadows as he went lower and lower. It was very quiet. Even his bare feet on the pavement made a mild echo.

Ram Singh continued downward until he reached a wide pool of sweet water. He filled his jars and climbed the steps with the lighter vessels. He could carry only one of the large vessels at a time. Suddenly, something moved above him; he looked up a saw a giant standing on the stairway. In one hand he had a dreadful looking mass of bones and in the other hand a lamp that cast long shadows on the walls. The giant asked him what he thought of his fair and lovely wife and held the light toward the bones in his arms while looking lovingly at them.

The poor giant had a very beautiful wife whom he had loved dearly; but when she died, he refused to believe that she was dead and carried her around long after she had become nothing but bones. Ram Singh of course did not know this, but he remembered the second saying of the guru, which forbade him to speak harshly or inconsiderately of others. Ram Singh told the giant that he was sure that the giant could find nowhere such a wife.

The giant told Ram Singh that he had good eyes and could see well. The giant said that he had slain many who had insulted his wife by saying that she was dried bones. He told Ram Singh that he was a fine young man and offered to help him. The giant set down the bones and picked up the two large vessels and carried them up the stairs, while Ram Singh carried the smaller ones.

The giant told Ram Singh that he had pleased him, and that he could ask a favor and it would be done. The giant asked him if he would like to be shown the buried treasure of the dead kings. Ram Singh shook his head at the mention of buried wealth and asked the giant if he would be willing to move on from haunting the well, so that men might go in and out to obtain water. The giant had expected a favor more difficult to fulfill, and his face brightened. He promised to leave at once. As Ram Singh went off through the gathering darkness with his precious burden of water, he saw the giant striding away with the skeleton of his dead wife in his arms.

There was great rejoicing in the camp when Ram Singh returned with the water. He didn't tell anyone about the giant. He merely told the rajah that there was nothing to prevent the well from being used. It was used frequently, and nothing more was seen of the giant.

The rajah was so pleased with Ram Singh that he ordered the vizier to give the young man to him in exchange for one of his servants. As the rajah's attendant, Ram Singh became more trusted eventually because, mindful of the guru's third counsel, he was always honest and spoke the truth. Ram Singh grew in favor and eventually the rajah made him treasurer, which provided him with wealth and power.

Unfortunately, the rajah had a brother known to be a bad man who had hoped to win the young treasurer over to himself, so that he could steal the rajah's treasure little by little. Then, with plenty of money, the brother planned to bribe the soldiers and some of the rajah's counselors and lead a rebellion to dethrone and kill his brother, so he could rule himself. The brother knew that he could not tell Ram Singh of his plans, so he began by flattering him and then by offering him his daughter's hand in marriage. Ram Singh respectfully declined the great honor of marrying a princess because he remembered the fourth piece of advice of the guru — never to try to appear the equal of those above him in station.

The rajah's brother was furious and was determined to bring about Ram Singh's ruin. He told the rajah that Ram Singh had spoken insulting words about his sovereign and his daughter. The rajah grew very angry and declared that until the treasurer's head was cut off, neither he nor his daughter nor his brother would eat or drink. However, the rajah didn't want anyone to know that he had ordered this, and said that anyone who mentioned it would be severely punished.

The rajah sent for an officer of his guard and told him to take some soldiers and ride to a tower just outside of town. If anyone came to ask when the building was to be finished or any other questions about it, the officer was to chop his head off and bury him on the spot. The officer thought that these instructions were odd, but it was no business of his. His business was to carry out orders.

Early the next morning the rajah, who had not slept all night, sent for Ram Singh and asked him to go to the new tower and ask how the construction was coming along and when it would be finished and then hurry back with the answer. As Ram Singh went down the road to the tower, he passed a small temple on the outskirts of the city and heard someone reading aloud. Remembering the guru's fifth counsel, he stepped inside and sat down to listen for a few minutes. He did not mean to stay longer, but he became more interested in the wisdom of the teacher as the sun rose higher and higher in the sky.

Meanwhile the wicked brother, who dared not disobey the rajah's command, became more and more hungry. His daughter cried waiting for news of Ram Singh's death so she could eat breakfast. Hours passed and no messenger arrived. At last the brother could wait no longer. He disguised himself so that he wouldn't be recognized, jumped on a horse, and rode out to the tower, where the rajah had told him that the execution was to take place. When he arrived, no execution was in progress. The men working on the tower were being watched by some idle soldiers.

The brother, forgetting that he had disguised himself, rode up and cried out asking the men why they weren't finishing what they had come to do. Then he asked when they would be done. The soldiers looked at the officer who gave them a signal. A sword flashed in the sun, and off flew the brother's head. A part of the brother's disguise was a thick beard, so the men didn't recognize the dead man as the rajah's brother. They rapped the head in a cloth and buried the body as they had been instructed. The officer took the cloth and rode back to the palace.

When the rajah returned to his quarters from a council meeting, he was surprised to find neither head nor brother waiting for him. He became uneasy and decided to go and see for himself what the matter was. He rode off alone and passed the temple where Ram Singh had stopped. Hearing hoofs, Ram Singh looked out and saw the rajah. Feeling ashamed for having forgotten his errand, he went out to meet his master. The rajah reined in his horse and was very surprised to see his treasurer.

At that moment, the officer arrived, carrying the parcel. He saluted the rajah gravely, dismounted, laid the bundle in the road, and began to unwrap it. When his brother's head was displayed to his view, the rajah dismounted and grabbed the officer by the arm. He questioned the officer as to what had occurred, and little by little a dark suspicion darted through him. He told the officer that he had done well and then questioned Ram Singh, who told him that, by listening to the guru's counsel, he had delayed pursuing the answer to the rajah's question.

The rajah found documents that proved his brother's treachery, and Ram Singh established his innocence. Ram Singh served the rajah for many years with unswerving loyalty. He married a maiden of his own rank in life, with whom he lived happily. He was loved by all men and honored upon his death. Sons were born to Ram Singh, and in time sons were born to them. He passed on to them the five wise sayings of the old guru.

Moral: We can learn from those older and wiser than ourselves.

Based on: Andrew Lang, "The Five Wise Words of the Guru,"
   The Olive Fairy Book

The Ditch-digger Falls into His Own Ditch

There once was a beggar who went from village to village to ask for alms. One village he visited regularly was very generous to him. When anyone gave him food or coins, he did not thank them but instead would say, "May you receive what you have given." Because of this phrase, everyone liked him and gave him all the more.

In the village that was especially kind to him lived two brothers-in-law who were rich merchants. Because they traveled frequently and were seldom at home, their wives were lonely. They began receiving men of the village in their homes. Whenever the two women gave to the beggar, he would say, "May you receive what you have given." The women, not realizing that he said this to everyone who helped him, took this greeting personally.

One sister said to the other, "Sister, we must get rid of that beggar. He knows of our affairs and will tell our husbands some day. Every time we give him anything, he says the same thing. Certainly he knows something that will bring us no good." The other sister agreed that it would not do for him to tell their husbands, and that they must get rid of him.

One day the sisters made coffee rolls and put poison in them. They added pretty decorations and made them as tempting as possible. Each took one to the beggar. The poor man thanked them in his usual way. The women were angry but said softly, "We shall see what you will receive."

That day the husbands of the two sisters rode past the beggar. One brother-in-law told the other that he was so hungry he couldn't possible ride home without food. The other brother-in-law said he was hungry, too, and suggested asking the beggar if he would sell them some of his bread. The beggar recognized the merchants, looked through his provision sack, and pulled out the two coffee rolls for the merchants. They threw the beggar some coins, ate the coffee rolls, and rode on.

45

Before long, one brother-in-law told the other that he felt sick. Something was wrong with his stomach, and he could barely stay on his horse. He suggested riding faster. The other brother-in-law said that he was ill, too, and had trouble breathing. When they reached their homes, they dismounted from their horses and collapsed. The wives called the healers and were told that their husbands had been poisoned. The healers asked them when they last ate and what they had to eat.

One of the merchants told of the beggar on the road. The healers questioned the beggar and were told that the two coffee rolls he had provided to the merchants had been given to him by their wives. The healers asked why they had given poisoned coffee rolls to the poor beggar. The wives were forced to admit their unfaithfulness and the reason that they wanted to get rid of the beggar. This is a case of the ditch-digger falling into his own ditch.

Moral: Do unto others as you would have them do unto you.

Based on: Susie Hoogasian-Villa, "The Ditch-digger Falls
            into His Own Ditch," *100 Armenian Tales*

The Man Who Stopped Going to Church

A tale from Scotland is about a man who lived long ago. God called him while he was still a young lad. Every day of his life he went to church and attended religious service. He did this for many years.

The man noticed that corn was disappearing from his stackyard. He went into the village to talk with the constable about it. The constable told him that if his corn was disappearing during the night, he should sit up all night and watch. Eventually, when he found out who was stealing it, the constable told him to come and report to him.

That night he saw a man come and lay a rope on the ground and pull sheaves out of the corn stack to make up a bundle. When he finished assembling the bundle, he carried it off. The man recognized the thief; it was the minister—the minister of his own church.

The man went back to his house. He never said a word to anyone, including the constable. When Sunday came and the townspeople went to church, the man just stood in his own doorway and watched them. He had not missed a day in church in over twenty years. That day he let everyone pass by him on their way to church.

A little later, the man took a Bible and walked up the glen. It was a fine summer day and he stretched out on the slope of the glen and began to read the Bible. After a while, he had the feeling that someone else was with him. He looked up and saw a man standing beside him looking down at him. The visitor saw that he was reading the Bible and asked him why he wasn't in church. He had never told anyone of what he had seen—a man stealing his corn—until now. He told the visitor the whole story and said that he was never going back to church. The minister was just a common thief and a bad man. He would never go to hear him preach again.

The visitor asked the man to come with him on a walk up the glen. When they were near the stream, a terrible thirst struck the man with the Bible. He was overcome by thirst and bent down and drank his fill from the stream. He was surprised at how refreshing it was. The visitor then asked him to walk further up the glen with him. Further up the glen, a dead horse was lying in the stream with a terrible smell coming from it—the smell of decay.

The visitor asked the man if he thought it strange that the water down below tasted so good. The visitor saw what the water was flowing through—a rotting carcass. The man with the Bible agreed that he had not noticed anything wrong with the water. It had tasted good. The visitor noted that that was the way of it, and that was the way of the Word and of the Gospel, too. It could not be sullied no matter what mouth it came out.

The visitor told the man that he shouldn't let what had happened to him keep him from going to church again. The visitor vanished and the man was left standing on the bank of the stream in deep thought.

Moral: As important as our communication with an intermediary
with a higher being is, our individual relationship with
our God is more important.

Based on: Alan Bruford and Donald A. MacDonald,
"The Man Who Stopped Going to Church,"
Scottish Traditional Tales

The Legend of the Lute Player

Centuries ago there were a king and queen who lived happily together. They were very fond of each other and had no worries. The king grew restless and wanted to go out into the world to try his strength against some enemy and to win honor and glory. The king called out his army and gave orders to advance to a distant country where a heathen king mistreated and tormented his subjects.

The king gave his parting orders and advice to his ministers and embarked with his army across the seas. When he reached the country of the heathen king, he marched on, defeating all who stood in his way. Eventually, he came to a mountain pass where a large army was waiting for him. The enemy defeated his army and took him prisoner.

The king was carried off to the prison where the heathen king kept his captives. The prisoners were chained together all night long and yoked together like oxen in the morning to plow the land all day until dusk. This went on for three years before the king found a way to communicate with his queen. He sent a message to her directing her to sell all their castles and palaces, to pawn all their treasures, and to come and rescue him from prison.

The queen received the message and wept bitterly, wondering how she could possibly rescue her husband. If she went herself, the heathen king would make her one of his wives. She didn't think any of her ministers were capable of succeeding. She thought long and hard and finally conceived of an approach. She cut off all her beautiful long brown hair and dressed in boys' clothes. Then she took her lute and ventured out into the world.

The queen traveled through many lands, saw many cities, and experienced many hardships before she reached the city of the heathen king. She walked around the palace and checked out the prison at the back of the structure. Then she went to the great court in front of the palace and began to play the lute so beautifully that the courtiers stopped what they were doing to listen. After playing for a while, she began to sing; her voice was sweeter than a lark's:

> I come from my own country far
> Into this foreign land
> Of all I own I take alone

My sweet lute in my hand.
Oh! Who will thank me for my song,
        Reward my simple lay?
Like lovers' sighs it still shall rise
        To greet thee by day.
I sing of blooming flowers
        Made sweet by sun and rain;
Of all the bliss of love's first kiss,
        And parting's cruel pain.
Of the sad captive's longing
        Within his prison wall,
Of hearts that sigh when none are nigh
        To answer to their call.
My song begs for your pity,
        And gifts from out your store,
And as I play my gentle lay
        I linger near your door.
And if you hear my singing
        Within your palace, sire,
Oh! Give, I pray, this happy day,
        To me my heart's desire.

When the heathen king heard this touching song sung by such a lovely voice, he had the singer brought before him. He welcomed the lute player and asked where he came from. The boy said that he was from far away across the sea, and that he had been wandering about the world for several years earning a living by singing and playing. The king asked the boy to stay for a few days and when the lute player was ready to leave, the king said that he would grant what was asked in the song—his heart's desire.

The lute player stayed on in the palace and sang and played all day long for the king, who never tired of listening and almost forgot to eat or drink or to torment people. He cared for nothing but the music. He said that it made him feel as though a gentle hand had lifted every care and sorrow from him. After three days, the lute player came to take his leave, and the king asked the boy what he desired as a reward.

The lute player asked for one of the king's prisoners. He told the king that he had so many prisoners he would not miss one, and that the prisoner would provide good company on the trip home. The king took the lute player to the prison himself where the queen dressed like a boy picked out her husband and took him with her on her journey. She led him nearer and nearer to their country; the king never realized who she was.

When they reached the frontier, the prisoner said, "Let me go now kind lad; I am no common prisoner but the king of this country. Let me go free and ask what you will as a reward."

"Do not speak of reward," answered the lute player. "Go in peace."

"Then come with me, dear boy, and be my guest."

"When the proper time comes, I shall be at your palace," he replied, and they parted.

The queen took the short way home, arrived at the palace before the king, and changed into a dress. An hour later, all the people in the palace were excitedly telling everyone that the king had returned. The king greeted everyone kindly but didn't pay much attention to the queen. He called his ministers and councilors together and told them what kind of wife he had. He said that here the queen hugged him, but that she had done nothing to help him when he was pining in prison and had sent word to her.

The council told the king that the queen had disappeared when she had received his message and had just returned that day. The king was very angry and told them to judge his faithless wife. He told the council that they would never have seen him again if a young lute player had not delivered him. He said that he would always remember the lute player with love and gratitude.

While the king was sitting with his council, the queen disguised herself again as the young lute player. She took her lute and went into the court in front of the palace and sang, clearly and sweetly:

> I sing the captive's longing
> > Within his prison wall,
> Of hearts that sigh when none are nigh
> > To answer their call.
> My song begs for your pity,
> > And gifts from out your store,
> And as I play my gentle lay
> > I linger near your door.

And if you hear my singing
Within your palace, sire,
Oh! Give, I pray, this happy day,
To me my heart's desire.

As soon as the king heard this song, he ran out to meet the lute player, took him by the hand, and led him into the palace. He told everyone in the court that this was the boy who had released him from prison. He told the lute player that he would indeed give him his heart's desire. The lute player told him that he was sure that the king would not be less generous than the heathen king, from whom he had obtained what he had requested.

The lute player said, "This time I don't intend to give up what I get. I want you—yourself!" At this point, the queen threw off her long cloak sand everyone saw that it was the queen. The king was overjoyed. He gave a great feast to the whole world, and the world came and rejoiced with him for an entire week.

Moral: Things aren't always what they appear. Occasionally
   support is received from the least-expected source.

Based on: Andrew Lang, "The Lute Player,"
The Violet Fairy Book

Chapter 3

SELF-DETERMINED / RESPONSIBLE

Oh! Much may be made by defying
    The ghosts of Despair and Dismay;
And much maybe gained by relying on
    "Where there's a will, there's a way."

Eliza Cook, "Where There's a Will, There's a Way."

The Green Door

Rudolf Steiner was a true adventurer. Most evenings he ventured out from his lodgings in search of the unexpected. To him, the most interesting thing in life was just around the corner. Sometimes his willingness to tempt fate had led him into strange paths. Twice he had to spend the night at the police station; repeatedly he had found himself the dupe of ingenious tricksters to whom he forfeited his watch and money. Nevertheless, he pursued every opportunity presented to him because it, hopefully, might lead to adventure.

One evening Rudolf was walking briskly along a crosstown street in an older section of the city. Two streams of people filled the sidewalks: those hurrying home and the restless contingent that abandons home for a fancy meal in a restaurant. The young adventurer had a pleasing appearance and moved watchfully. He was a salesman in a piano store.

Rudolf walked by a restaurant that had an eye-catching sign out front with large teeth on it. He wondered about this until he saw a dentist's sign on the second floor above the restaurant. A giant, gaudily dressed African American distributed cards to those in the passing crowd who would take them. Rudolf was familiar with this method of advertising, and he usually managed to walk by without taking one. However, the African American slipped one into his hand very deftly.

Rudolf walked a few yards before he looked at the card. One side of the card was blank, and the words, "The Green Door," were handwritten on the other side. He saw the man in front of him throw down the card that he had been handed. Rudolf picked it up. The dentist's name and address were printed on the card along with a promise of "painless" dentistry.

The adventurous piano salesmen stopped at the corner, hesitated, and then retraced his steps past the restaurant. When he walked past the African American, Rudolf took the card handed to him. Ten paces later he looked at it and found the same handwritten words, "The Green Door," on it. He picked up four cards that had been discarded in the street. Every one bore the name and address of the dentist.

Rudolf walked back to where the African American was standing. This time he was not handed a card but was given a look of disdain by the man. This contemptuous look stung the adventurer. He read in the look a silent accusation that he had been found wanting. Whatever the mysterious written words might mean, he had been selected twice to be given them and now was considered somehow deficient to receive them.

Rudolf stood back from the building and noticed signs above the dentist's for palmists, dressmakers, musicians, and doctors. Above these signs in the five-story building were curtains in the windows of apartments. He walked briskly up the stone steps to the building. The first three floors had a carpeted stairway. Above those floors the hallway was dimly lit. On the first floor of apartments, he saw a green door. He hesitated and then walked up to the green door and knocked.

The moments that passed before his knock was answered provided an anticipation of the unknown that he had experienced before. He could be confronted by gamesters at play, rogues baiting their traps, danger, disappointment, or ridicule. A faint rustle was heard inside, and the door slowly opened. A girl, barely twenty, stood there, white-faced and tottering. She let go of the doorknob and swayed weakly, groping with one hand. Rudolf caught her and laid her on a faded couch that stood against the wall. He closed the door and looked around the room in the dim light. He observed neat but extreme poverty.

The girl lay still, as if in a faint. Rudolf began to fan her with his hat. Unintentionally, he struck her nose with the brim of his derby, and she opened her eyes. The young man saw that her face was the one missing from his heart's gallery of intimate portraits. The frank, gray eyes, the little nose, which turned pertly upward, the chestnut hair, curling attractively, seemed to be the reward for all his adventures. However, the face was woefully thin and pale. The girl looked at him calmly and smiled.

"Fainted, didn't I?" she asked, weakly. "Well, who wouldn't? Try going without anything to eat for three days and see!" Rudolf exclaimed an oath, jumped up, and told her to wait until he came back. He dashed through the green door and down the stairs.

He was back in twenty minutes kicking at the door for her to open it. Both arms were full of food from the nearby grocery store and restaurant. On the table, he laid out the wares: bread and butter, cold meat, cakes, pickles, oysters, roast chicken, milk, and hot tea.

Rudolf took a cup from a shelf by the window and filled it with tea. The first thing she reached for was a large dill pickle, which he had to take from her. He told her to start with a small glass of milk, then the tea, and then a chicken wing. He said that she could have a pickle tomorrow, and that if she would give him permission to be her guest, they would have supper.

Rudolf drew up another chair. The tea brightened the girl's eyes and brought back some of he color. She ate with a sort of dainty ferocity like a starved animal. She seemed to regard the young man's presence and the aid he had rendered as a natural thing—not that she undervalued conventions, but as one whose great stress had given her the right to put aside the artificial for the humane.

Gradually, with the return of her strength, came also a sense of the little conventions that remained, and she told him her story. It was one of a thousand stories in the city every day—the shop girl's story of insufficient wages, further reduced by "fines" to swell the store's profits; of time lost through illness; and then of lost positions; lost hope—and finally the knock of the adventurer on the green door. Rudolf commiserated with her on her experiences. She admitted that it had been very difficult.

Rudolf asked her if she had any relatives or friends in the city, and she said that she didn't. When he told her that he was alone in the world, too, she said that she was glad to hear that. Somehow it pleased him that she approved of his parentless condition. Suddenly her eyelids dropped, and she sighed.

Rudolf rose, took his hat, and said good night. He told her that a good night's sleep would do her good. He held out his hand; she took it and said good night to him. Her eyes asked a question so pathetically that he answered it with words. He told her that he would come back tomorrow to see how she was getting along. He told her that she could not get rid of him that easily.

When Rudolf reached the door, she asked him how he had come to knock on her door. He looked at her and wondered what would have happened if the cards had fallen into the hands of another type of adventurer. He quickly decided that she must never know the truth about what had driven him to respond to her great distress. He told her that his piano tuner lived in the building, and that he had knocked on her door by mistake. The last thing he saw in the room before the green door closed was her smile.

At the head of the stairway, Rudolf paused and looked curiously around him. Puzzled, he went to the other end of the hallway and then up to the next floor. Every door that he found in the building was painted green. When he reached the sidewalk, he went over to the African American and asked why he had been given those two particular cards and what they meant. With a broad, good-natured grin, the man pointed down the street. Rudolf looked in that direction and saw, above the entrance to a theater, the blazing electric sign for its new play, "The Green Door."

The African American told Rudolf that he heard it was a first-rate show, but that he was a bit late for the first act. He told Rudolf that the agent for the play had paid him to distribute cards for the play along with the dentist's.

At the corner of the block where Rudolf lived, he stopped at a bar for a glass of beer and a cigar. When Rudolf had finished his beer, he came outside with his lighted cigar, buttoned his coat, pushed back his hat, and said to the lamppost on the corner, "All the same, I believe it was the hand of Fate that guided the way for me to find her." This conclusion, under the circumstances, certainly admits Rudolf Steiner to the ranks of the true followers of Romance and Adventure.

Moral: We cannot depend on chance or luck, but we can
       take advantage of it when it presents itself.

Based on: O. Henry, "The Green Door," *The Four Million*

The Cannon That Wasn't Fired

The story of the cannon that wasn't fired is also the story of the nomination of Abraham Lincoln in 1860 at the Republican National Convention in Chicago. The convention opened on May 16 at the Wigwam, a building erected for the occasion. The large New York delegation, including political boss Thurlow Weed, Governor King, and a delegation of respected businessmen and lawyers, arrived in Chicago on May 12.

William H. Seward, who was favored to win the nomination, stayed home in Auburn and let his team wage the battle for him. On May 17, everything seemed arranged for Seward's nomination. The

New York delegation sent him a telegram on the morning of May 18: "Everything indicates your nomination today sure." After receiving that message, Seward's friends moved a six-pounder brass cannon into the street next to his home. They planned to move the cannon into the small park adjoining the grounds of Seward House and to fire it in celebration when news of his nomination was received.

On the first ballot, Seward received 173 and 1/2 votes, and Lincoln received 102; the rest of the votes were scattered, with many states voting for their favorite sons. Seward received 184 and 1/2 votes to Lincoln's 181 on the second ballot. Seward received 180 votes on the third ballot, and Lincoln received 231 and 1/2. Nomination required 233.

Then D. K. Carter, chairman of the Ohio delegation, stood and announced the shift of four of Ohio's votes to Lincoln, and the rail-splitter was nominated. Horace Greeley, editor of the New York *Herald Tribune* and a foe of the Seward forces, gloated; Thurlow Weed, realizing that his friend Bill Seward would never be President of the United States, buried his face in his hands and wept.

The New York delegation sent another telegram to Seward: "Lincoln nominated third ballot." With no change of facial expression, Seward said, "Well, Mr. Lincoln will be elected and has some of the qualities to make a good President." The defeated nominee's friends removed the small cannon from the street adjacent to his home; it was not to be fired in celebration of Seward's victory after all.

Several factors contributed to Lincoln's victory and Seward's defeat. Lincoln's campaign managers, including David Davis, out-maneuvered Thurlow Weed by promising cabinet positions for votes. Lincoln had instructed his team to make no commitments in his name, but he fulfilled the promises that were made on his behalf.

Seward had stated that the abolition of slavery would take a long time, but that it would happen. He was viewed as more of an extremist on slavery than Lincoln. Even in his "A House Divided Cannot Stand" speech, Lincoln had advocated moderation. Other delegates were concerned that Seward would be influenced in the White House by political bosses to a greater extent than Lincoln.

William H. Seward was a capable individual who would have made a good President. However, Lincoln went on to become, in the opinion of historians, the greatest President in United States history.

Moral: Don't count your chickens before they are hatched.

Emerson Klees, "The Cannon That Wasn't Fired,"
Legends and Stories

The King Who Would See Paradise

Long ago there was a king who, one day when he was out hunting, encountered a fakir in a lonely place in the mountains. The fakir, who wore a patched cloak thrown over his shoulders, was seated on an old bedstead reading the Koran.

The king asked the fakir what he was reading. The fakir replied that he was reading about Paradise and praying that he might be able to enter there. The king asked the fakir if he could show him a glimpse of Paradise, because he found it difficult to believe in what he could not see.

The fakir told the king that he was asking a very difficult and perhaps very dangerous thing. The fakir added that he might be able to do it if he prayed for the king. He warned the king against the danger of his lack of belief and against the curiosity that prompted him to make this request. However, the king was not to be dissuaded. He promised to give the fakir food, if he, in return, would pray for him. The fakir agreed, and they parted.

Time passed, and the king provided food to the fakir as promised; however, whenever the king asked when the fakir was going to show him Paradise, the answer was always, "Not yet, not yet!"

After two years had gone by, the king heard that the fakir was very ill—indeed, possibly dying. The king hurried to the fakir's bedside and found that it was true; the fakir was near his last breath. The king asked him to remember his promise to show him a glimpse of Paradise.

The dying fakir told the king to come to his funeral, and, when the grave had been filled in and everyone had gone away, to lay his hand upon the grave; then the fakir would keep his word and show him a glimpse of Paradise. Nevertheless, he implored the king not to do this, but to be content to see Paradise when God called him there. Nevertheless, the king's curiosity was so strong that he still wanted to do it.

After the fakir died and was buried, the king stayed behind until everyone had left the cemetery. Then he knelt down and placed his hand on the grave. Instantly, the ground opened, and the astonished king saw a flight of rough steps. At the bottom of them, the fakir was sitting, just as he used to sit, on his rickety bedstead reading the Koran!

At first the king was so surprised and frightened that he could only stare. The fakir beckoned to him to come down. Mustering his courage, the king boldly stepped down into the grave. The fakir rose and, motioning for the king to follow him, walked a few paces along a dark passage. Then he stopped, turned solemnly to his companion, drew aside a heavy curtain, and revealed—what?

No one knows what was shown to the king, nor did he ever tell anyone. When the fakir closed the curtain, the king turned to leave the place; he had his glimpse of Paradise! Trembling in every limb, the king staggered back along the passage and stumbled up the steps out of the grave into the fresh air.

Dawn was breaking. It seemed odd to the king that he had been so long in the grave. It seemed to have been just a few minutes ago that he had descended, walked a few steps to the place where he had looked beyond the curtain, and returned after perhaps five minutes of that wonderful view! And what had he seen? He racked his brains and could not remember a single thing.

The king gazed around him. Everything seemed changed. He was entering his own city, but it looked different and strange to him. The sun was already up when he turned into the palace gate and entered the public reception hall. It was full, and another king sat upon the throne. The poor king was bewildered; he sat down and looked around. A chamberlain came up to him and asked why he sat unbidden in the king's presence. He cried out, "But I am the king!"

The chamberlain asked, "What king?"

"The true king of this country," he said indignantly.

The chamberlain went away and spoke to the king on the

throne; the old king heard words like "mad," "age," and "compassion." The king on the throne called him to come forward, and as he did, he saw his reflection in the polished shield of the king's bodyguard and stepped back in horror. He was old, decrepit, and ragged. His long white beard and hair straggled unkempt all over his chest and shoulders. The only sign of royalty that remained to him was the signet ring on his right hand. He pulled it off with shaking fingers and held it up to the king.

"Tell me who I am," he cried. "Here is my signet ring, who once sat where you sit—even yesterday!"

The king looked at him compassionately and examined the ring with curiosity. He asked for the dusty records and archives of the kingdom to be brought out and examined. After the records had been reviewed, the king turned to the old man and said," Old man, such a king as the one whose signet you have reigned seven hundred years ago. He disappeared, and no one knew where he had gone. Where did you get this ring?"

The old man struck his breast and cried out with a loud lamentation. He understood that he, who had not been content to wait patiently to see the Paradise of the faithful, had been judged already. He turned and left the hall without a word and went up into the mountains, where he lived a life of prayer and meditation for twenty-five years. At last, the Angel of Death came for him and mercifully released him, purged and purified through his punishment.

Moral: Be careful what you ask for; you might get it.

Based on: Andrew Lang, "The Story of the King Who
        Would See Paradise," *The Orange Fairy Book*

The Legend of Prince Ahmed al Kamel

There once was a Moorish king of Granada who had a son, Ahmed, to whose name the king's courtiers added the surname of al Kamel, the perfect, from the signs of excellence they perceived in him in his infancy. The astrologers predicted everything in his favor that could make a perfect prince and a prosperous sovereign. Only one cloud overshadowed his destiny: he had an amorous temperament and was subject to the perils of tender passion. If he could be kept from the allurements of love until he attained maturity, these dangers could be averted and his life could be one of uninterrupted happiness.

To prevent danger of this kind, the king decided to rear the prince in seclusion, where he would never see a female face nor hear about love. For this purpose he built a beautiful palace, the Generalife, on the brow of the hill above the Alhambra, in the middle of well-tended gardens surrounded by lofty walls.

The youthful prince was shut up there and entrusted to the guardianship and instruction of Eben Bonabben, one of the wisest Arabian sages, who had spent most of his life in Egypt studying hieroglyphics and conducting research on the pyramids. The sage was directed to instruct the prince in all kinds of knowledge but one — to keep him ignorant of love. The king commanded that if his son learned about that forbidden knowledge, Bonabben would lose his head. The sage assured the king that he could rest easy; he was not about to give lessons about idle passion.

Under the vigilant care of the philosopher, the prince grew up in the seclusion of the palace and its gardens. Black slaves attended upon him — mutes who knew nothing of love, or if they did, could not communicate it. Bonabben initiated Ahmed into the lore of Egypt. The prince made little progress in that subject and in philosophy, however. He obtained a smattering of knowledge and reached his twentieth year, still totally ignorant of love.

About this time a change came over the prince. He abandoned his studies and began to stroll in the gardens and muse by the fountains. He devoted his time to music and poetry. Bonabben tried to distract the prince with algebra, which the student disliked. The prince said that he wanted a subject that spoke more to the heart. The sage was concerned that his pupil had learned that he had a heart. Bonabben feared that the latent tenderness of the prince required only an object.

The young man wandered around the gardens of the Generalife with feelings that he didn't understand. Sometimes he would sit in reverie; then he would pick up his lute and play sentimental notes before throwing the instrument aside and sighing. The loving disposition of the prince began to extend to inanimate objects, such as favorite flowers. Bonabben was alarmed by his pupil's excited state and had him shut up in the highest tower of the Generalife.

The sage searched his mind for subjects that might interest the prince. Finally, he remembered that when he was in Egypt, he had been instructed in the language of birds by a rabbi. The prince welcomed instruction in the subject, and before long he was as adept at talking to birds as his teacher. The tower was no longer a place of solitude; he had companions with whom he could converse.

One of the prince's first acquaintances was an owl, a wise-looking bird with a large head and staring eyes, who sat all day in a hole in the wall but ventured out at night. He claimed to be wise, talked about astrology and the moon, and hinted at the dark sciences and metaphysics. The prince found him to be almost as ponderous as Bonabben.

Another acquaintance was the swallow, with whom the prince was initially impressed. He was a smart talker but restless, bustling, and always on the wing; he seldom remained long enough in one place for extended conversation. He turned out to be one that skimmed over the surface of things, pretending to know everything but knowing no subject thoroughly.

Winter passed, spring opened with all its bloom, and the happy time arrived for birds to pair and build their nests. Suddenly, song burst forth from the gardens of the Generalife and reached the prince in the solitude of his tower. From every side he heard the same universal theme—love—love—love—burst forth. The prince listened in silence and perplexity. He wondered, "What can be this love of which the world seems so full, and of which I know nothing?"

The prince asked the owl to tell him what this love was about which all the birds in the groves below were singing. The owl put on a look of offended dignity. He said that his nights are taken up with study and research and his days with reflection. He told the prince that he didn't listen to the other birds. He was a philosopher who knew nothing of this thing called love.

The prince talked to the swallow to find out what could be learned from him. As always, the swallow was in a hurry and had little time to reply. He said that he had much public business to attend to and no time to think about the subject. He told the prince that he was a citizen of the world and knew nothing of this thing called love.

Finally the prince decided to ask his ancient guardian about the one subject about which he had received no instruction. He said, "Tell me, oh most profound of sages, what is the nature of this thing called love?" Bonabben was struck as by a thunderbolt, and he trembled and turned pale. He asked the prince where he had learned such an idle word.

The prince led the sage to the tower window and told him to listen. The nightingale sat in a thicket below the tower singing to his paramour. From below rose the strain of love—love—love. The wise Bonabben exclaimed, "Who shall pretend to keep this secret from the heart of man, when even the birds of the air conspire to reveal it?"

The sage told the prince, "Shut your ears to these seductive strains; close your mind against this dangerous knowledge. Know that this love is the cause of half the ills of humanity. It is what produces strife between brethren and friends and causes treacherous murder and desolating war. It is accompanied by care and sorrow and weary days and sleepless nights. It withers the bloom, blights the joy of youth, and brings on the grief of premature old age. Allah preserve you, my prince, in total ignorance of this thing called love."

Bonabben went to bed, leaving the prince in even deeper perplexity. The prince listened to the strains of the birds and heard no sorrow in their notes; everything seemed tenderness and joy. If love were a cause of such wretchedness, why weren't the birds drooping in solitude or tearing each other to pieces, instead of fluttering cheerfully around the groves?

The prince lay one morning on his couch, meditating on this matter. The window of his chamber was open to admit the soft morning breeze, which carried the perfume of orange blossoms from the valley of the Darro River. The voice of a nightingale was heard and, with a sudden rushing noise, a beautiful dove, pursued by a hawk, darted in the window and fell panting on the floor, while its pursuer flew off to the mountains.

The prince picked up the gasping bird, smoothed its feathers, and nestled it on his chest. Then he soothed it, placed it in a golden cage, and offered it food. The bird refused the food and sat drooping, pining, and uttering piteous moans. When asked what ailed him, the dove told the prince that he was sad because he had been separated from the partner of his heart in the happy spring-time, the season of love.

The prince asked the dove to tell him about love. The dove told him that it was the torment of one, the happiness of two, and the strife of three. It is the charm that draws two beings together and unites them by delicious sympathies, making it happiness to be with each other but misery to be apart.

The dove asked the prince if there was anyone to whom he was drawn by ties of tender affection. The prince admitted that there were only his friends. The dove told him, "That isn't the sympathy I mean. I speak of love, the great mystery and principle of life, the intoxicating revel of youth, and the sober delight of old age. Look outside, my prince and see how at this season all nature is full of love. Every being has its mate; the most insignificant bird sings to its paramour; the beetle woos its lady beetle in the dust. The but-terflies you see fluttering high above the tower are happy in each other's loves. My prince, have you spent so many of the precious days of youth without knowing anything of love? Is there no gen-tle being of the other sex—no beautiful princess or lovely damsel who has captured your heart and filled you with tender thoughts?"

"I begin to understand," said the prince, sighing. "Such a feel-ing I have more than once experienced, without knowing the cause. Where could I seek such a one as you describe in this place of dis-mal solitude?"

The prince said that if love were such a delight and its inter-ruption such misery, he would not confine the dove. He opened the cage and took the bird to the window and released him. He encour-aged the dove to rejoice with the partner of his heart in the days of youth and springtime. He said that he would not make him a fellow prisoner in a dreary tower where love can never enter. The dove flew away and swooped downward to the banks of the Darro.

The prince confronted the sage Bonabben: "Why have I been kept in complete ignorance, and why has the great mystery and principle of life been withheld from me when the meanest insect knows about it? All nature is in a revel of delight. Every being rejoices with its mate. This is the love about which I have sought instruction. Why am I alone restricted from its enjoyment? Why has so much of my youth been wasted without a knowledge of love's raptures?"

The sage Bonabben saw that all further hesitation was useless. The prince had acquired the dangerous and forbidden knowledge. He told the prince about the predictions of the astrologers, and the precautions that had been taken in his education to prevent the threatened evils. The tutor pointed out to the prince that his own life was now in the prince's hands. If the king found out that the prince had learned about the passion of love, Bonabben would lose his head. The prince agreed to keep the realization to himself rather than endanger the life of his guardian.

A few mornings later, the prince was standing out on the battlements of the tower, when the dove that he had released alighted fearlessly on his shoulder. Ahmed fondled the bird and asked where he had been since they had parted.

"In a far country, my prince, from where I bring you tidings in reward for my liberty. In my flight, which extended over plain and mountain, I saw below a delightful garden with all kinds of fruit and flowers. It was in a green meadow on the banks of a wandering stream. A stately palace was in the center of the garden. I came down to rest after my weary flight.

"On the green bank below me was a youthful princess, in the very sweetness and bloom of her youth. She was surrounded by female attendants, young like herself, who decked her with garlands of flowers. No flower or garden could compare with her for loveliness. However, she bloomed in secret, for the garden was surrounded by high walls, and no mortal man was permitted to enter. When I saw this beautiful and innocent maid, I thought here is the being formed by heaven to inspire my prince with love."

This description was the spark to ignite the combustible heart of Ahmed. All the latent desire of his temperament had found an object, and he conceived an unmeasurable passion for the princess. He wrote a letter in the most passionate language stating his fervent devotion, but bemoaning his unhappy bondage, which prevented him from visiting her and throwing himself at her feet. He added couplets of the most tender and moving eloquence, for he was a poet by nature and inspired by love. He addressed his letter—"To the Unknown Beauty, from the captive Prince Ahmed." Then he perfumed it with musk and roses and gave it to the dove.

The dove soared high in the air and flew in one undeviating direction. The prince followed him with his eye until he was a mere speck. Day after day he watched in vain for the return of the messenger of love. Toward sunset one evening, the dove fluttered into his chamber and expired at his feet. The arrow of some cruel archer had pierced his breast, yet the dove had struggled on to fulfill his mission. The prince bent with grief over the gentle martyr and saw a chain of pearls around his neck with a small picture attached. It was of a lovely princess in the flower of her years.

It was doubtless the unknown beauty of the garden, but who and where was she? How had she received his letter? Was this picture sent as a token of her approval of his passion? Unfortunately the death of the dove left everything in doubt. The prince gazed at the picture for hours. He wondered where in this wide world he could find the original. Potential lovers might be crowding around her while he was a prisoner in the tower adoring a mere picture.

The prince resolved to leave the palace, which had become his prison. To escape from the tower during the daytime would be difficult; but at night the palace was lightly guarded. No one would expect an attempt of this kind from the prince, who had been passive in his captivity. He wondered how he could find his way and thought of the owl, who was accustomed to roam at night. The owl self-importantly claimed to have knowledge of all the towers, fortresses, and citadels in Spain. He said if there was some knowledge of castles and palaces that he didn't have, then his brother, uncle, or cousin did.

The prince described his mission to the owl, who was not interested in helping the prince. The owl's research and meditation took precedence. The prince promised any reward that he chose. The owl told him that he didn't need anything other than a few mice a day. Fortunately, the owl was ambitious. The prince told him that one day he would be the sovereign and could place the owl in a position of honor and dignity. The owl immediately promised to be the prince's guide and mentor on his pilgrimage.

The prince collected all his jewels to use as traveling funds. That night he lowered himself by a rope of scarfs from a balcony of the tower, climbed over the walls of the Generalife, and, guided by the owl, escaped into the mountains. The owl suggested that Ahmed begin his search in Seville. The owl's uncle used to live in ruined wing of the Alcazar there. When visiting the uncle, the owl frequently saw a light burning in a lonely tower. The tower was occupied by an Arabian magician and an ancient raven who had come with the magician from Egypt. The magician had died, but the raven still inhabited the tower. The owl suggested that the prince consult the raven, who was a soothsayer and a conjurer dealing in the black arts.

The prince took the owl's advice and headed for Seville. Traveling only at night, one morning they reached Seville. The owl rested in a tree while the prince entered the gate to the city and found the Giralda, the famous Moorish tower of Seville. The prince climbed the great winding staircase to the summit of the tower where he found the raven—an old, mysterious, gray-headed bird with ragged feathers and a film over one eye. He was standing on one leg studying a diagram on the floor.

The prince approached the raven with reverence and asked if he could interrupt his studies to request his help in locating the object of his passion. He showed the raven her picture and asked if where she could be found was within the scope of the raven's knowledge. The raven said that his visits were to the old and withered, and that he had little knowledge of youth and beauty. He suggested that the prince look elsewhere.

The prince told the raven that he was a royal prince, fated by the stars and sent on a mysterious enterprise on which might hang the destiny of empires. At that, the raven changed his tone and suggested that the prince go to Cordova and seek the palm tree of the great Abderahman, which stands in the courtyard of the principal mosque. At the foot of the tree, the prince would find a great traveler who had visited all countries and courts and had been a favorite of queens and princesses. He would provide information about the object of the search. The prince thanked the raven for the information and went on his way.

The prince and the owl set off for Cordova, which they approached through hanging gardens and orange and citron groves overlooking the valley of the Guadalquivir River. When they arrived at the city gates, the owl found a hole in the wall in which to perch, and the prince looked for the palm tree planted by the great Abderahman. It stood in the middle of a great courtyard surrounded by orange and cypress trees. Dervishes and fakirs were seated in groups under the cloisters.

At the foot of the palm tree, the crowd's attention was attracted by one particular speaker. The prince thought that this must be the great traveler who would know the princess, until he saw that the crowd was listening to a parrot. The prince asked a bystander why so many serious people would listen to a chattering bird. The bystander told him that the parrot was a descendant of the famous parrot of Persia, renowned for his storytelling talent. He had all the learning of the East at the tip of his tongue and could recite poetry as well as he could talk. Also, he had visited many foreign courts, where he was considered a prodigy of erudition.

The prince arranged a private meeting with the parrot. He showed him the portrait and asked if he had encountered the princess in the course of his travels and his visits to castles and palaces. The parrot told the prince that it was the picture of the Princess Aldegonda, one of his favorites, and that she was the only daughter of the Christian king who reigned in Toledo. The parrot told Ahmed that she was shut up from the world until her seventeenth birthday because of a prediction of those meddlesome fellows, the astrologers. The prince was told that he wouldn't be able to meet her; no mortal man was allowed to see her.

The prince immediately left Cordova for Toledo with the parrot, picking up the owl from his hole in the wall on the way through the city gates. The birds had a tendency to bicker; one was a wit and the other a philosopher. They traveled through the passes of the Sierra Morena, across the plains of La Mancha, and along the banks of the "Golden Tagus."

Eventually they came within sight of Toledo, which had walls and towers built on a rocky promontory encircled by the Tagus River. The owl spoke of the antiquities of the city, but the parrot said that he preferred to talk of an abode of youth and beauty and pointed to the home of the princess. It was a stately palace surrounded by a garden set in a green meadow on the banks of the Tagus.

The prince saw that the walls of the garden were of great height, with armed guards patrolling them. Realizing that he didn't have access to the garden but the parrot did, the prince asked the parrot to be his emissary to tell the princess of his arrival. The parrot flew over the walls and alighted on the balcony of a pavilion that overhung the river. He saw the princess reclining on a couch reading a letter, while tears rolled down her pale cheeks.

The parrot perched beside the princess and told her to dry her eyes because he had come to console her. The princess was startled on hearing a voice. When she saw the little green-feathered bird, she asked what consolation he could possibly provide. He told her that Ahmed, the prince from Granada, had arrived in Toledo and was currently encamped on the banks of the Tagus. The eyes of the princess sparkled at this news; she said that she had been faint and weary, sick almost unto death, with doubt about Ahmed's interest in her. She asked the parrot to tell Ahmed that the words of his letter were engraved on her heart, and that his poetry had been the food of her soul.

The princess instructed the parrot to tell Ahmed that he must prepare to prove his love by force of arms. She said that tomorrow was her seventeenth birthday and her father the king was holding a great tournament. Several princes were to enter the lists, and her hand would be the prize to the victor.

The parrot relayed the message to the prince. Ahmed's happiness at finding the princess was tempered by news of the impending tournament. In fact, the banks of the Tagus were already glittering with arms and resounding with trumpets of the knights traveling to Toledo to attend the tournament. The same star that had controlled the destiny of the prince had governed that of the princess, and until her seventeenth birthday she had been shut away from the world to guard her from tender passion. Several powerful princes had contended for the hand of Princess Aldegonda. Her shrewd father, rather than making enemies by showing partiality, referred them to the arbitration of arms. Several of the rivals were known for their strength and prowess.

This was a predicament for the unfortunate Ahmed who was unprovided with weapons and unskilled in the exercise of chivalry. Brought up in seclusion under the eye of a philosopher, he was totally lacking in the knowledge of arms. The owl exclaimed, "God is great! In his hands are all secret things—he alone governs the destiny of princes! Know, oh prince, that this land is full of mysteries, hidden from all but those who, like myself, can grope after knowledge in the dark. Know that in the neighboring mountains there is a cave, and in that cave there is an iron table, and on that table there lies a suit of magic armor. A magic lance leans on the table, and nearby stands a spell-bound steed, all of which have been shut up for many generations."

The prince stared in wonder, while the owl blinked his huge, round eyes, lifted his head, and proceeded. "Many years ago I accompanied my father to these parts on a tour of his estates, and we stayed in that cave; thus I became acquainted with the mystery. This armor belonged to a Moorish magician, who took refuge in the cave when Toledo was captured by the Christians. He died there, leaving the steed and weapons under a mystic spell, never to be used but by a Moslem, and by him only from sunrise until midday. During that interval, whoever uses them will overthrow every opponent."

Ahmed suggested that they immediately look for the cave, which they found in one of the wildest recesses of the rocky cliffs. An owl was one of the few creatures that could have found the entrance. As the owl had said, the armor lay on an iron table in the center of the cavern. The lance leaned against it, and beside it was the Arabian steed, ready to take the field. The armor was as bright and gleaming as the last time it had been used. The steed was in good condition and neighed joyfully when Ahmed laid his hand upon its neck. Despite his lack of experience, the prince was determined to take on the field in the tournament.

The eventful morning arrived. The lists for the combat were prepared in the Vega, or plain, just below the walls on the cliffs of Toledo, where galleries had been erected for spectators, covered with rich tapestries and sheltered from the sun by silken awnings. The beauties of the land were assembled in those galleries, while below pranced plumed knights with their pages and squires. All the beauties of the land were eclipsed when the Princess Aldegonda appeared in the royal pavilion and for the first time was seen by an admiring world.

The princess impressed the crowd with her loveliness, but she had a troubled look. The color came and went from her cheeks and she turned a curious eye with an dissatisfied expression over the throng of plumed knights. The trumpets had sounded for the encounter when the herald announced the arrival of a strange knight.

Ahmed rode onto the field. A steel helmet studded with gems rose above Ahmed's turban; his breastplate was embossed with gold. His scimitar and dagger gleamed with precious stones. He had a round shield at his shoulder, and his right hand held the lance that never lost. The trappings of his Arabian steed were richly embroidered, and the proud animal pranced, sniffed the air, and whinnied when it saw the array of arms.

The lofty and graceful demeanor of the prince caught every eye and when his title, "The Pilgrim of Love," was announced, there was a universal flutter among the ladies in the galleries. However, when Ahmed presented himself at the lists, they were closed to him. He was told that none but princes were admitted to the contest. He declared his name and rank. That made his prospects worse—he was a Moslem and could not engage in a tourney where the hand of a Christian princess was the prize.

The rival princes surrounded Ahmed. One of the more insolent among them sneered at his youth and scoffed at his amorous title. The prince's ire was aroused, and he challenged his rival to an encounter. They took their positions, wheeled, and charged. At the first touch of the magic lance, the brawny scoffer was tilted from his saddle. The prince should have paused here, but he was contending with a demoniacal horse and armor; once in action, nothing could control them. The Arabian steed charged into the throng; the lance overturned everyone there.

The gentle prince was carried about the field, strewing it with the high and low, the gentle and simple, and horrified by his lack of control. The king fumed at this outrage on his subjects and guests. He ordered out all his guards; they were unhorsed as soon as they entered the field. Finally, the king threw off his robes, grabbed his shield and lance and rode forth to awe the stranger with the presence of majesty itself. Unfortunately he fared no better than his predecessors. To Ahmed's dismay, he was borne full tilt against the king and in a moment the royal heels were in the air, and the crown was rolling in the dust.

At this moment, the sun reached its peak and the magic spell lost its power. The steed galloped across the plain, leaped over the barrier, plunged into the Tagus, swam in its raging current, and bore the prince breathless and amazed to the cavern, where the stallion resumed his station, like a statue, next to the iron table. The prince was relieved to dismount and replace the armor on the table.

Ahmed thought about the desperate state to which the demoniacal steed and armor had reduced him. He would never dare to show his face in Toledo after inflicting such a disgrace upon its chivalry and such an outrage on its king. What would the princess think of his rude and riotous achievement? He sent out his winged messengers to gather news. They returned with a world of gossip. All Toledo was in consternation.

The princess had been carried off senseless to the palace. The tournament had ended in confusion. Everyone was talking of the sudden appearance, prodigious exploits, and strange disappearance of the Moslem knight. Some thought he was a Moorish magician, others considered him a demon in human form, and still others talked about enchanted warriors hidden in caves in the mountains.

The owl went out at night and flew to the palace. When he returned in the morning, he told the prince that he had looked through a window and had seen the princess. She was reclining on a couch surrounded by attendants and physicians, but she would have none of their ministrations. When they left, she withdrew a letter from her bosom and read it and kissed it, accompanied by loud lamentations. Ahmed was distressed at this news.

Further information from Toledo corroborated the report of the owl. The princess had been conveyed to the highest tower of the palace, and every approach was heavily guarded. A deep melancholy had seized her. She refused food and turned a deaf ear to every attempt to console her. The most skillful physicians were mystified; no one could determine the cause for her melancholy. It was thought that some magic spell had been cast upon her. The king made a proclamation that whoever could cure her would receive the richest jewel in the royal treasury.

When the owl heard of the proclamation, he observed that the man who effected the cure of the princess would be happy if only he knew what to choose from the royal treasury. Ahmed asked the owl what he meant. The owl mentioned that he knew of a college of antiquarian owls that held their meetings in the tower where the royal treasury was kept. They evaluated the various gems, jewels, and gold and silver vessels. They were mainly interested in the old relics and talismans in the treasury. Among these was a box of sandalwood secured by steel bands of Oriental workmanship and inscribed with mystic characters. An ancient owl from Egypt proved that the box contained the silken carpet of the throne of Solomon, which had been brought to Toledo by Jews who took refuge there after the fall of Jerusalem.

When the owl finished talking of his antiquarian friends, Ahmed was deep in thought. He said, "I have heard from the sage Bonabben of the wonderful properties of that talisman, which disappeared at the fall of Jerusalem and was supposed to have been lost to mankind. Doubtless it remains a sealed mystery to the Christians of Toledo. If I can get possession of that carpet, my future is secure."

The next day the prince laid aside his rich attire and arrayed himself in the simple garb of an Arab of the desert. He dyed his complexion a tawny hue; no one would recognize him as the warrior who had caused such trouble at the tournament. He presented himself at the gate of the royal palace and announced that he was a candidate for the reward offered for the cure of the princess. The guards were going to drive him away, asking what a vagrant Arab could do when the king's physicians had failed. However the king had overheard the conversation and asked for the Arab to be brought to him.

The king knew of the wonderful secrets possessed by the Arabs and was inspired with hope by the confident words of the prince. The king conducted him immediately to the lofty tower at the top of which were the chambers of the princess. The windows opened upon a terrace with a commanding view of Toledo and the surrounding countryside. The prince seated himself on the terrace and played several Arabian airs on his pastoral pipe that he had learned from his attendants at the Generalife. Then the prince laid aside the reed and, to a simple melody, chanted the amatory verses of the letter that declared his passion.

The princess recognized the verses and joy entered her heart; she raised her head and listened. Tears streamed down her cheeks, and her bosom rose and fell with a tumult of emotions. The king asked the minstrel to enter the chambers of the princess. The lovers were discreet. They exchanged mere glances, but those glances spoke volumes. The rose had returned to the cheeks of the princess, the freshness to her lips, and the light to her eyes. The physicians were astonished, and the king regarded the Arab minstrel with admiration.

The king asked Ahmed what he would like from the royal treasury. Ahmed replied that it would not be gold, silver, or precious stones; his choice was a relic handed down from the Moslems who had once owned Toledo—a sandalwood box containing a silken carpet. Ahmed said that if he were given that box, he would be content. Everyone was surprised at the moderation of the choice of the Arab, particularly when the box was brought out and the carpet withdrawn. It was of fine green silk, covered with Hebrew and Chaldaic characters.

The prince told them that the carpet had once covered the throne of Solomon; it was worthy of being placed beneath the feet of beauty. Ahmed spread it on the terrace beneath the ottoman that had been brought for the princess and then sat at her feet and said, "Who shall counteract what is written in the book of fate? Behold the prediction of the astrologers verified. Know, oh king, that your daughter and I have loved each other in secret. Behold in me the Pilgrim of Love!"

These words had barely left his lips when the carpet rose in the air, bearing off the prince and the princess. The king and the physicians gazed at it until it became a speck on the horizon. The king raged at his treasurer. He asked how he had allowed an infidel to get possession of such a talisman. The treasurer admitted that they had not been able to translate the inscription on the box and had no idea of its contents.

The king assembled a mighty army and set off for Granada. His march was long and toilsome. They camped in the Vega, and he sent a herald demanding restitution of his daughter. The King of Granada himself came forth with his court to meet him. Then the King of Toledo beheld the real minstrel, for Ahmed had succeeded to the throne on the death of his father, and the beautiful Aldegonda was his sultana.

The Christian king was easily pacified when he learned that his daughter had been allowed to continue in her faith. Instead of a bloody battle, there was a succession of feasts and rejoicings, after which the king returned satisfied to Toledo, and the young couple reigned happily and wisely in the Alhambra.

Ahmed appointed the owl and the parrot as his counselors, as he had agreed to do. They provided him with valuable advice in administering the realm.

Moral: Be determined and persistent and you will achieve
    your goals, even without magic.

Based on: Washington Irving, "The Legend of Prince Ahmed
    al Kamel," *The Alhambra*

The Legend of the Promise

Margarita, her face hidden in her hands, was weeping. She did not
sob, but tears ran silently down her cheeks, slipping between her
fingers to fall to the earth toward which her brow was bent. Near
Margarita was Pedro, who from time to time lifted his eyes to steal
a glance at her and, seeing that she still wept, dropped them again,
maintaining for his part utter silence.

All was hushed about them, as if everything was respecting her
grief. The murmurs of the field were stilled, the breeze of evening
slept, and darkness was beginning to envelop the dense growth of
the wood. Moments passed, during which the trace of light that the
dying sun left on the horizon faded away. The moon was faintly
sketched against the violet twilight sky, and the brighter stars shone
through.

At last Pedro broke the distressful silence, exclaiming in a
hoarse voice as if he were communing with himself, "It is impossible—impossible!" Then, coming close to the inconsolable maiden
and taking one of her hands, he continued in a softer, more caress-
ing tone.

"Margarita, for you love is all, and you see nothing beyond
love. Yet there is one thing as binding as our love, and that is my
duty. Our lord the Count of Gomara goes forth tomorrow from his
castle to join his forces to the army of King Fernando, who is on his
way to deliver Seville from the Moors, and it is my duty to go with
the Count.

"An obscure orphan, without name or family, I owe to him all
that I am. I have served him in the idle days of peace, I have slept
beneath his roof, and I have been warmed at his hearth and eaten at
his table. If I forsake him now, tomorrow his men-at-arms, as they
march out of the castle gates, will ask, wondering at my absence,
'Where is the favorite squire of the Count of Gomara?' And my lord
will be silent for shame, and his pages and his fools will say in

mocking tone, 'The Count's squire is only a gallant of the jousts, a warrior in the game of courtesy.'"

After her lover had spoken, Margarita lifted her eyes full of tears to meet his and moved her lips as if to answer him, but her voice was choked in a sob. Pedro, with a still tenderer and more persuasive tone, continued, "Do not weep, Margarita; do not weep. Your tears hurt me. I must leave you, but I will return as soon as I have gained a little glory for my obscure name. Heaven will aid us in our holy enterprise. We shall conquer Seville, and to the conquerors the King will give fiefs along the banks of the Guadalquivir River. Then I will come back for you, and we will go together to dwell in that paradise of the Arabs, where they say the sky is clearer and more blue than the sky above Castile. I will come back; I swear to you I will. I will return to keep the troth solemnly pledged to you that day when I placed on your finger this ring, symbol of a promise."

"Pedro!" exclaimed Margarita, controlling her emotion and speaking in a firm, determined tone, "Go, go to uphold your honor," and on saying these words, she threw herself for the last time into the embrace of her lover. Then she added, in a tone lower and more shaken, "Go to uphold your honor, but come back to save mine."

Pedro kissed Margarita's brow, untied the reins of his horse from one of the trees in the grove, and rode off at a gallop through the poplar trees. Margarita followed Pedro with her eyes until his dim form was swallowed up by the shades of night. When he could no longer be seen, she went back to the village where her brothers were waiting for her. When she returned home, one of her brothers told her to set out her gala dress because in the morning they were going to Gomara with all the neighbors to watch the Count march off to Andalusia.

Margarita answered with a sigh that, for her part, it saddened rather than gladdened her to see those go who might not return. Her other brother insisted that she come with them and remain composed, so that the gossiping folk would have no cause to say that she had a lover in the castle, and that her lover went to war.

Hardly was the first light of dawn breaking across the sky when the shrill trumpeting of the Count's soldiers sounded throughout the camp of Gomara. Peasants arrived from the surrounding region and looked up at the multicolored banners flapping in the wind from the highest tower of the fortress.

The peasants were everywhere—seated on the edge of the moat, ensconced in the tops of trees, strolling over the plain, on the crests of the hills, and forming a line along the highway. They had waited for over an hour and were beginning to get impatient when the bugle call sounded, the chains of the drawbridge creaked as it fell slowly across the moat, the portcullis was raised, and the massive doors of the arched passage that led to the Court of Arms swung aside.

The multitudes pressed for places on the sloping banks along the road to see the brilliant armor and sumptuous trappings of the followers of Count Gomara, famed throughout the countryside for his splendor and his lavish pomp. The march was opened by the heralds who, halting at fixed intervals, proclaimed in loud voice, to the beat of the drum, the commands of the King, summoning his subjects to the Moorish war and requiring the villages and free towns to give passage and aid to his armies.

After the heralds followed the kings-at-arms, proud of their silken vestments, their shields bordered with gold and bright colors, and their caps decked with graceful plumes. Then came the chief retainer of the castle, a knight mounted on a young black horse, bearing in his hands the banner of a grandee with his motto and device; at his left hand rode the executioner of the fortress, clad in black and red. The steward was preceded by a score of the famous trumpeters of Castile known for the incredible power of their lungs.

When the mighty clamor of their trumpeting ceased, a dull sound, steady and monotonous, could be heard—the tramp of foot soldiers, armed with long pikes and carrying leather shields. Behind them came the soldiers who managed the engines of war, with their crude machines and wooden towers, and the bands of wall scalers along with the stable boys in charge of the mules.

Then, enveloped in a cloud of dust raised by the hoofs of their horses, flashing reflections from their iron breastplates, passed the men-at-arms of the castle, formed in dense platoons, from a distance looking like a forest of spears. Last of all, preceded by drummers mounted on strong mules decked out in bright covers and plumes, surrounded by pages in rich raiment of silk and gold, and followed by the squires of the castle, appeared the Count.

As the multitudes caught sight of him, a great shout of greeting went up. In the tumult of acclamation was stifled the cry of a woman, who at that moment, as if struck by a thunderbolt, fell fainting into the arms of those nearby who sprang to her aid. It was Margarita, who had recognized her lover. Her Pedro was no squire, but that great and dreadful lord, the Count of Gomara himself, one of the most exalted and powerful lords of the Crown of Castile.

Months later, the host of King Fernando, after going north from Cordova, had marched to Seville by fighting its way through Ecija, Carmona, and Alcala del Rio del Guadaira, whose famous castle, taken by storm, put the Christian army in sight of the stronghold of the Moors. The Count of Gomara was in his tent seated on a wooden bench, motionless, pale, disconsolate, his hands crossed upon the hilt of his broadsword, his eyes fixed in space with that vague regard that appears to behold a specific object but observes nothing in the surrounding scene.

Standing by his side, the squire who had been longest in the castle, the only one who in those moods of black despondency could venture to intrude without drawing down upon himself an explosion of wrath, asked him, "What ails you, my lord? What trouble wears and wastes you? You are sad going into battle, and you are sad returning, even though you are victorious. When all the warriors sleep, surrendering to the weariness of the day, I hear your anguished sighs. If I run to your bed, I see you struggling against some invisible torment. You open your eyes, but your terror does not vanish. What is it, my lord? Tell me. If it is a secret, I will guard it in the depths of my memory as in a grave."

The Count seemed not to hear his squire, but after a long pause, as if the words had taken all that time to make the slow way from his ears to his understanding, he emerged little by little from his trance. Drawing the squire affectionately toward him, he said gravely, "I have suffered much in silence. Believing myself the sport of a vain fantasy, I have until now held my peace for shame — but no, what is happening to me is no illusion. I must be under the power of some awful curse. Heaven or hell must wish something of me and tell me so by supernatural events. Do you recall the day of our encounter with the Moors of Nebriza in the Aljarafe de Triana? We were few, the combat was fierce, and I was face to face with death. You saw how, in the most critical moment of the fight, my horse, wounded and blind with rage, dashed toward the main body of Moors. I tried in vain to check him. The reins had dropped from my hands, and the fiery animal galloped on, bearing me to certain death.

"Already the Moors, closing their ranks, were holding their pikes to receive me on the points; a cloud of arrows hissed about my ears. The horse was but a few lengths from the spears on which we were about to fling ourselves, when—believe me, this was not an illusion—I saw a hand that, grasping the bridle, stopped him with an unearthly force and, turning him in the direction of my own troops, saved me by a miracle. In vain, I asked everyone around me who my deliverer was. No one knew him; no one had seen him.

"'When you were rushing to throw yourself upon the wall of pikes,' they said, 'you went alone, absolutely alone; this is why we marveled to see you turn, knowing that the steed no longer obeyed his rider.'

"That night I entered my tent distraught; I tried in vain to erase the memory of the strange adventure. On moving toward my bed, I again saw the same hand, a beautiful hand, white to the point of pallor, that drew the curtains, vanishing after it had drawn them. Ever since, at all hours, in all places, I see that mysterious hand that anticipates my desires and forestalls my actions. I saw it, when we were storming the castle of Triana, catch between its fingers and break in the air an arrow that was about to strike me. I have seen it at banquets where I was trying to drown my trouble in revelry, pour wine into my cup. It always flickers before my eyes, and wherever I go it follows me: in the tent, in battle, by day, by night—even now, see it here, resting on my shoulder."

The Count sprang to his feet and walked back and forth as if beside himself, overwhelmed by utter terror. The squire brushed away a tear. Believing his lord mad, he did not try to question his ideas but restricted himself to saying in a voice of deep emotion, "Come. Let us go out from the tent for a moment; perhaps the evening air will cool your temples and calm this incomprehensible grief, for which I can find no words of consolation."

The camp of the Christians extended over all the plain of Guadaira, even to the left bank of the Guadalquivir River. In front of the camp and clearly defined against the bright horizon, rose the walls of Seville flanked by massive, menacing towers. Above the crown of battlements showed in its rich profusion the green leaves of the thousand gardens enclosed in the Moorish stronghold, and amid the dim clusters of foliage gleamed the observation turrets, the minarets of the mosques, and the gigantic watchtower.

The enterprise of King Fernando, one of the most heroic and intrepid men of his time, had drawn to his banners the greatest warriors of the kingdoms in the peninsula and others who had come from foreign lands to add their forces to his.

Stretching along the plain were army tents of all forms and colors, above whose peaks waved in the wind the various ensigns with their escutcheons — stars, griffins, lions, chains, bars and cauldrons, with hundreds of other heraldic figures and symbols that proclaimed the name and quality of their owners. Through the streets of that improvised city circulated in all directions a multitude of soldiers who, speaking in diverse dialects, dressed in the fashion of their own locale and armed according to their fancy, formed a scene of strange contrasts.

A group of nobles rested from the fatigues of combat on wooden benches at the door of their tent playing chess, while their pages poured them wine in metal cups. Some soldiers took advantage of a moment of leisure to mend and clean their armor. Further on, the most expert archers of the army were covering a target with arrows, amidst the applause of an admiring crowd. Peddlers could be heard hawking their wares, mingled with the sound of iron striking on iron. Minstrels singing ballads could also be heard entertaining their audience by relating prodigious exploits. The air was filled with the thousands of discordant noises surrounding an army at rest.

The Count of Gomara, attended by his faithful squire, passed among these lively groups without raising his eyes from the ground. He was silent and sad, as if no sight disturbed his gaze nor sound reached his hearing. He moved mechanically as a sleepwalker whose spirit was busy in the world of dreams and who was unconscious of his actions as if driven by a will not his own.

Near the royal tent and in the middle of a ring of soldiers, pages, and camp servants, was an odd personage, half pilgrim, half minstrel. One moment he recited a litany in bad Latin and the next moment engaged in buffoonery accompanied by devout prayers and jests that made the common soldier blush. He intermixed romances of illicit love with legends of the saints. He was also a peddler who sold things such as Gospels sewed into small silk bags, relics of the patron saints of all the towns in Spain, tinsel jewels, chains, sword belts, medals, and items made of brass, glass, and lead.

When the Count approached the group formed by the pilgrim and his admirers, the fellow began to tune a mandolin. When he had thoroughly tested his strings, he announced the title of the ballad and sang in a monotonous and plaintive voice. The stanzas all ended with the same refrain.

The Count listened attentively. By a strange coincidence, the title of the ballad was the subject of the melancholy thoughts that burdened his mind. The title was "The Ballad of the Dead Hand." The squire, on hearing so strange a title, tried to draw his lord away; however, the Count remained motionless with his eyes fixed on the minstrel.

> A maiden had a lover gay
> Who said he was a squire.
> The war drums called him far away;
> No tears could quench his fire.
> "Thou goest to return no more."
> "Nay, by all oaths that bind."
> But even while the lover swore,
> A voice was on the wind:
> *Ill fares the soul that sets its trust*
> *On faith of dust.*

> Forth from the castle rode the lord
> With all his glittering train,
> But never will his battle sword
> Inflict so keen a pain.
> "His soldier honor well he keeps;
> Mine honor—blind! oh, blind!"
> While the forsaken woman weeps,
> A voice is on the wind:
> *Ill fares the soul that sets its trust*
> *On faith of dust.*

Her brother's eye her secret reads;
    His fatal angers burn.
"Thou hast shamed us." Her terror pleads,
    "He swore he would return."
"But to find thee, if he tries,
    Where he was wont to find."
Beneath her brother's blow she dies;
    A voice is on the wind:
Ill fares the soul that sets its trust
    On faith of dust.

In the trysting wood, where love made mirth,
    They have buried her deep—but lo!
However high they heap the earth,
    A hand as white as snow
Comes stealing up, a hand whose ring
    A noble's troth doth bind.
Above her grave no maidens sing,
    But a voice is on the wind:
Ill fares the soul that sets its trust
    On faith of dust.

The singer had hardly finished the last stanza, when the Count pushed through the wall of eager listeners, clutched the singer's arm, and whispered in a low, agitated voice, "From what part of Spain are you?"

"From Soria," was the calm response.

"And where did you learn this ballad? Who is the maiden of the story?" asked the Count with even more emotion.

"My lord," said the pilgrim, fixing his eyes upon the Count imperturbably, "This ballad is passed from mouth to mouth among the peasants of Gomara, and it refers to an unhappy village girl cruelly wronged by a great lord. The high justice of God has permitted that, in her burial, there shall remain above the earth the hand on which her love placed a ring in plighting her his troth. Perhaps you know who is bound to keep that pledge."

According to legend, the strange ceremony of the Count's marriage took place in a wretched village on one side of the highway leading to Gomara. He knelt upon the humble grave and pressed the hand of Margarita in his own. When a priest blessed the mournful union, the miracle ceased and the dead hand buried itself forever. At the foot of some great old trees nearby is a meadow that spontaneously covers itself with flowers every spring. The country folk say that this is the burial place of Margarita.

Moral: Promises should be kept. The consequences of not
       fulfilling a promise can be grim.

Based on: Gustavo Adolfo Becquer, "The Promise,"
       Romantic Legends of Spain

Chapter 4

PERSEVERING / RESOURCEFUL

When things go wrong, as they sometimes will,
When the road you're trudging seems all uphill,
When care is pressing you down a bit,
Rest, if you must—but don't you quit.
Often the goal is nearer than
It seems to a faint and faltering man,
Often the struggler has given up
When he might have captured the victor's cup.

Author unknown

Diamond Cut Diamond

In a village in Hindustan there once lived a merchant who, although he rose early, worked hard, and went to bed late, was very poor. He moved to another country to try to improve his luck. After twelve years passed, his luck had turned; he had accumulated great wealth, enough to keep him in comfort for the rest of his life. Once more he thought of his native village, where he wanted to spend the remainder of his life among his own people.

In order to carry his riches with him in safety over the many miles to his village, he bought some magnificent jewels, which he locked up in a small box that he concealed upon his person. To avoid drawing the attention of thieves who infested the highways, he dressed in the poor clothes of a man who had nothing to lose.

He traveled quickly and within a few days' journey of his village came to city where he could buy better garments. Now that he was no longer afraid of thieves, he wanted to look more like the rich man that he had become. In his new clothes, he found a bazaar that was finer than all the other shops filled with the goods of all countries. The owner, who had displayed his goods to their best advantage, sat smoking a long silver pipe.

The merchant greeted the owner politely and made some purchases. Beeka Mull, the owner of the shop, was a very shrewd man, and as he and the merchant conversed, he concluded that his customer was richer than he seemed and was trying to conceal the fact. After the purchases were made, Mull invited the traveler to refresh himself, and soon they were chatting pleasantly. Mull asked the merchant where he was traveling, and, hearing the name of the village, advised him to be careful on that road because it was a bad place for thieves.

The merchant paled at these words. He thought that it would be unfortunate to be robbed at the end of his journey of the fortune that he had accumulated with such care. He thought that the prosperous Mull must know what he was talking about. The merchant asked Mull if he would lock up a small box for him until he reached his village and brought back a half dozen sturdy kinfolk to reclaim it. Mull told him that he could not do it. Such things were not his business, he said, and he would be afraid to undertake it. The merchant said that he knew no one else in the city, that he must have some place safe to keep his precious things, and that Mull would be doing him a great favor.

Mull still politely refused. The merchant continued to press him, until at last Mull consented. The merchant gave him his small box of jewels and Mull locked it up in his strongbox with other precious stones. The merchant left and visited some of the other shops in the bazaar to make small purchases and to inquire about Mull's reputation. Virtually every shop owner in the bazaar was a thief, and Mull was the biggest of them all; nevertheless, the shop owners all replied in praise of Mull as a model of virtue.

With the merchant's concerns satisfied, he left for his home village. A week later he returned to the city with a half dozen nephews whom he had enlisted to help him carry home the precious box. The merchant left his nephews at the great marketplace and went to retrieve the box of jewels. He greeted Mull, who pretended not to see him. He greeted him again and was asked what he wanted. The merchant asked Mull if he remembered him, and the shopkeeper said that he didn't. Why should he? He didn't remember every beggar who came begging for charity.

The merchant began to tremble. He mentioned that surely Mull remembered him as the one who gave him the small box for safekeeping. Mull called him a scoundrel and ordered him out of his shop. He said that everyone knew that he didn't store valuables for people. He said that he had enough trouble safeguarding his own precious items. Two other shopkeepers helped Mull throw the merchant out of the shop.

The merchant knew that he was ruined. He slumped down against a wall and drowned in self-pity. At about eleven o'clock, an enterprising young fellow named Kooshy Ram walked by with a friend and wondered who would be sitting against the wall in the dark. On his way home at five o'clock in the morning Ram passed by again and saw, to his astonishment, that the man had not moved. Ram went over to the merchant and asked him what was wrong, and if he were ill.

The merchant said that he was ill from an ailment for which there was no medicine. Ram answered that he could come up with a medicine that would cure him. Ram took him to his home, gave him food and a large glass of wine, and asked the merchant to tell his story.

When the merchant didn't come back to the marketplace, his

nephews returned to their village. The high-spirited, good-hearted Ram decided to help the merchant. If the shrewd young man hadn't come to the merchant's aid, he would have had no one to help him. Ram laughed that anyone would entrust wealth to Mull, for Ram knew him as the greatest rascal in the city. Ram repeated that he knew just the medicine to cure the merchant's illness.

A few days later Ram asked some friends to visit. They talked for a long time, and the merchant could hear them laughing among themselves. The next day Ram asked the merchant to go to the place in the bazaar where he had sat slumped against the wall. Ram directed him when he saw the signal to go up to Mull and ask him again to return the small box of jewels. The merchant asked what was the use; Mull wouldn't respond any better than he had the last time. Ram told him to do it anyway.

As he slumped against the wall, the merchant saw a gorgeous covered litter like those in which ladies of rank are transported. It was carried by four bearers dressed in rich liveries, and its curtains and trappings were truly magnificent. In attendance was a serious-looking person whom the merchant recognized as one of Ram's friends. Behind him was a servant with a box on his head that was covered with a cloth. The litter was set down at Mull's shop. Mull was on his feet at once and bowed as the gentleman in attendance walked up to him.

Mull inquired who was in the litter that favored his humble shop with a visit. The gentleman explained that she was a relative of his who was traveling. Since her husband could go no further with her, she wished to leave with Mull a box of jewels for safe-keeping. Mull said that this was not quite in his line of business, but if he could be of service to the lady, he would be happy to help. He added that he would guard the box with his life. The servant carrying the box was called up. The box was unlocked, and a large quantity of jewelry was shown to Mull, whose mouth watered as he turned over the loose gems.

As the merchant watched from a distance, he saw a hand motion to him from inside the covered litter. He wondered if this were the signal. When it beckoned again, he decided that it must be. The merchant went over to Mull and asked if he could have the box of jewels back that he had left in trust with him. Mull looked as though he had been stung but then realized that if he made a fuss, he would lose the confidence of this new and richer customer. Mull cried that he had forgotten all about the box and quickly agreed to return it. He got the box and placed it in the merchant's trembling hands. The merchant unlocked his box and checked its contents, which were all there. He ran down the road, dancing and laughing.

Just then a messenger ran up the road and told the gentleman attending the litter that the lady's husband had returned and planned to travel with her. There was no longer any need to deposit the jewels. The gentleman quickly closed the box and handed it back to the waiting servant. A yell of laughter came from the covered litter and out jumped—not a lady—but Ram, who immediately joined the merchant in the middle of the road and danced as madly as he.

Mull stood and stared stupidly at them; then he tore off his turban and joined them in dancing and laughing. The gentleman accompanying the litter asked Mull why he was dancing. He could see that the merchant danced because he had recovered his fortune. Ram danced because he was the madman who had tricked you, but why did he dance?

Mull replied that he danced because he knew of thirteen ways to deceive people by gaining their confidence in him. He didn't realize that there were any more. Now he had learned a fourteenth!

Moral: Trust your fellow man, but only within reasonable doubt.

Based on: Andrew Lang, "Diamond Cut Diamond,"
    The Olive Fairy Book

The Crumb in the Beard

Years ago there was a king who had a daughter named Stella. She was indescribably beautiful but so whimsical and hard to please that she drove her father to distraction. Princes and kings had sought her hand in marriage, but she found defects in all of them. As she grew older, her father became concerned about to whom he could leave his crown. He summoned his council to discuss the matter. The council advised the king to give a great banquet, to which he should invite all the princes and kings of the surrounding countries. There must be, among so many, someone who would please the princess. She could hide behind a door and examine them all in private.

The king gave the orders to arrange the banquet. He told Stella about his plans, and said that he hoped to find someone to please her. After all, his hair was white, and he must have someone to whom to leave his crown. Stella said that she would try to do as he wished.

The princes and kings arrived at the court. When it was time for the banquet, they seated themselves at the large table. The hall was beautifully adorned and a fountain flowed in all four corners of the hall. Gold and silver shone from the necks of the princes and kings. Wine flowed freely.

While the gentlemen were at dinner, Stella and one of her maids stood behind the door observing them. The maid pointed out a prime candidate, but Stella thought that this nose was too big. Another one had eyes that looked like saucers. The one at the head of the table had too large a mouth and looked as though he liked to eat too much. Stella found fault with all but one, whom she said pleased her, except that he must be a very dirty fellow because he had a crumb on his beard after eating.

The young man heard Stella say this and swore in vengeance. He was the son of the King of Green Hill and the handsomest youth in the crowd. When the guests had departed, the king called his daughter and asked if she had anything to tell him. She admitted that the only one who pleased her was the one with the crumb in his beard, but she thought that he must be a dirty fellow and did not want him. The king told her to take care, and that she might be sorry.

Stella's chamber overlooked a courtyard into which opened a baker's shop. One night when she was preparing for bed, she heard, from the room where they sifted meal, a man singing so well and with so much grace that it went to her heart. She ran to the window and listened until he had finished singing. She asked her maid to find out who the singer was. Stella could not wait until the next day to find out. Her maid told her that it had been the sifter.

That evening Stella heard him sing again, and she stood by the window until everything grew quiet. The voice had so touched her that she had to see who had that fine voice. In the morning she placed herself by the window and saw the youth come into the shop. As soon as she saw him, she was enchanted by his good looks and fell desperately in love with him.

This young man was none other that the prince at the banquet whom Stella had called "dirty." He had disguised himself and was plotting his revenge. After he had seen her once or twice, he took off his hat to salute her. She smiled at him and appeared at the window whenever he was around. They began to exchange words, and in the evening he sang under her window.

When Stella told him that she was unmarried, he began to court her, and he asked her to marry him. She consented at once but asked what he had to live on. He admitted that he didn't have a penny, and the little that he earned was barely enough to support himself. Stella encouraged him and told him that she would provide the money to support them.

To punish Stella for her pride, her father and the prince's father had an understanding and pretended not to know about the love affair. The king let Stella carry away from the palace all that she owned. Each day, Stella assembled a bundle of clothes, silver, and money, and at night she threw it down from the balcony to the disguised prince. After she had given him most of her possessions, finally he told her that it was time to elope. That night, she tied a cord around herself and let herself down to the ground.

The prince led Stella to a nearby city, where he turned down a street and opened the first door he came to. They went down a long passageway and came to a little hole-in-the-wall room that had only one window, high up on the wall. The room was furnished with a straw bed, a bench, and a dirty table. Stella looked around and thought that she would die.

The prince asked Stella what was the matter. He reminded her that he had not deceived her, and that she had known that he was poor. He told her that he had used the bundles she had given him to pay his debts. He said that she must make up her mind to work to earn her bread as he did. He told her that he was a porter for the king, and that he often went to work at the palace. Tomorrow they had work for him, so Stella must rise early and come along. The prince told her that he would set her to work with the other women. When the other servants went home for dinner she should say that she was not hungry. While she was alone, she must steal two shirts, hide them under her skirt, and carry them home.

Poor Stella wept bitterly, saying that it was impossible for her to do that. Her husband demanded that she do it, or he would beat her. The next morning the prince rose with the dawn and made her get up too. He made her wear a striped skirt and a pair of coarse shoes. He went with her to the palace and took her to the laundry, where he introduced her as his wife and left her. He told Stella to remember what awaited her at home if she disobeyed him. Then the prince ran and dressed himself like a king and waited at the palace gate until it was time for her to leave work.

Meanwhile poor Stella did as her husband had ordered and stole the shirts. As she was leaving the palace, she met the king, who asked her if she were the porter's wife. He then inquired what she had under her skirt.

When she refused to answer, he shook her until the shirts dropped out. The porter's wife is a thief, he sneered. Stella ran home, crying all the way. Her husband had arrived home ahead of her and put on his disguise. Stella told him what had happened and pleaded with him not to send her to the palace again.

The prince told Stella that the next day they were to bake. She must help in the kitchen and steal a piece of dough. Everything happened as on the previous day. Stella's theft was discovered, and when her husband returned home he found her crying like a condemned soul. She told him she would rather die than go to the palace again.

The prince told Stella that the king's son was to be married the next day, and a great banquet was to be held. She must wash dishes in the kitchen, and when the opportunity presented itself, she must steal a pot of broth and hide it about her so that no one would see it. She did as she was told and had barely concealed the pot when the king's son came into the kitchen and told Stella that she must come to the ball that followed the banquet. She did not want to go but he took her by the arm and led her into the midst of the festival.

Imagine how Stella felt at the ball, dressed as she was, and with the pot of broth! The king poked his sword at her in jest, until he hit the pot and the broth ran all over the floor. Everyone jeered and laughed, until poor Stella fainted from shame. When they had revived her, the prince's mother stepped forward and told her son that this was enough, he had avenged himself sufficiently.

Turning to Stella, the prince's mother said, "Know that this is your mother, and that the prince has done this to temper your pride and to be avenged for your calling him dirty." Then she took Stella into another room, where a maid dressed her as a queen. Stella's father and mother then appeared and kissed and embraced her. Her husband begged her pardon for what he had done; they made peace and always lived in harmony. From that day on she was never haughty; she had learned the lesson that pride is one of the greatest faults.

Moral: Pride goeth before a fall.

Based on: Stith Thompson, "The Crumb in the Beard,"
One Hundred Favorite Folktales

The Three Words of Advice

Once there was tinsmith who was out of work. Fearing that his family would starve, he said to his wife, "Wife, I can find no work here and we shall die of hunger. I must go abroad; it may be that there my luck will change, and we too shall be turned towards the face of God. As I wish to see you again, look well after our child. Now knead up a little maize flour and make me a few biscuits, and let me go off with God's blessing." His wife did as requested, and he departed.

The man went on his way and after ten days came to a large city. He looked for a job everywhere and finally found work on a farm. He worked hard, and after fifteen years he told his master that he wanted to return home. His master gave him two hundred gold pieces and sent him on his way.

The man was already on the road when his master called out to him to come back for some advice. His master asked for ten gold pieces for the advice, however. The tinsmith took ten gold pieces out of his pocket to pay for it. His master said, "Never mix yourself up in other people's affairs; you have seen nothing, and you know nothing."

The man again said good-bye but was again asked to stop. The master offered another piece of advice for another ten gold pieces. The man handed over the gold pieces and asked for the advice. The master said, "Never leave the king's highway." The man said good-bye and started down the road. The master stopped him again to offer one last piece of advice. The man grumbled under his breath that soon his master would have all the money back, but he paid the final ten gold pieces. His master told him, "First think and afterwards act." The man bid his master a final good-bye.

On the road he met a young man, and they traveled together. They spent the evening at an inn. The innkeeper had no room, so he put them up in the stable, where three Persian horses munched on their barley. The two men lay down on the straw and went to sleep. They were awakened at midnight overhearing three men who were getting the horses ready to ride. One of the riders said, "There are three hours left before dawn. Let us get down the road quickly in time to cut in front of them. At the big turn in the road we shall be in time to catch the guards with their load of treasure." The men mounted and set out down the road.

The young man suggested to the tinsmith that they tell the innkeeper what they had heard. The tinsmith advised him to go back to sleep and not to get mixed up in other people's business. He told the young man that he had neither seen nor heard anything. It was no affair of theirs.

The young man went in and informed the innkeeper, who was part of the gang. Afraid the youth might tell someone else, the innkeeper seized him and hanged him from the tree across the road. In the morning the tinsmith awoke and saw that his companion had been murdered. As he walked down the road, the tinsmith was thankful that he had paid his master ten gold pieces for the first piece of advice.

The tinsmith walked on and met two camel drivers with ten camels loaded with Persian shawls and silk cloth. They traveled together, and eventually they became hungry. The camel drivers said that they knew of a large inn off the king's highway. They suggested going there to eat and then returning to the highway. The tinsmith told them that he would not leave the king's highway, but that he would wait for them to return. The camel drivers left the camels with the tinsmith and went to the inn.

Before long, the tinsmith heard a noise like thunder, and the ground shook. He asked other travelers what had happened and was told that the inn had a store of gunpowder and cartridges. A fire had been lit, and somehow sparks had traveled to the gunpowder. The inn and everybody in it had been blown up. So the camels were left with the tinsmith. What could he do? It was the will of God. He took the camels and moved on.

Ten days later he came to his house. The night was dark as pitch. He walked up to the door and peered in through a crack. He saw his wife and a fine young man sitting by the fire. At first, he suspected something. In a rage he took out his gun to kill the youth. At that moment, he remembered the third piece of advice. He lowered the gun and considered who the youth might be. As he was thinking, he heard the youth say, "Mother, in the morning I shall go to the fields. Set the food by the fireside and go and fetch a load of wood."

She said, "Very well, I will go and fetch wood, my dear, but as for food, what am I to do? We have nothing here to cook. Your father, my darling, went off abroad; he is lost and has forgotten all about us."

The son said, "What shall we do, mother, do you ask? God is good, and He will not forget us." At that moment his father opened the door and with tears flowing rushed into the house and embraced them and kissed them. From that time on, they lived happily.

Moral: Recognize good advice when it is given and act upon it.

Based on: Stith Thompson, "The Three Words of Advice," *One Hundred Favorite Tales*

The Legend of the White Slipper

Once upon a time there was a king with a striking fifteen-year-old daughter. Even the mothers with daughters of their own admitted that the princess was more graceful and beautiful than any of them. Among the fathers, the princess was a subject of constant admiration.

King Balancin had been a complete slave to his little girl from the moment he lifted her from the arms of her dead mother. He did not seem to realize that there was anyone else in the world to love. Princess Diamantina had many proposals of marriage before she was fifteen, but her father turned all of her suitors down.

Behind the palace a large garden extended to foothills lining a river valley. Early every evening, the princess, attended by her ladies, strolled through the garden, gathering flowers for her rooms. When she finished, she walked through the town to talk to the people, who told her their troubles. She then returned to the palace and consulted with her father about the best way to help those who needed it.

King Balancin love to hunt. He spent several mornings a week hunting boars in the mountains north of the town. One day while running downhill chasing a boar, he stepped into a hole and fell into a pit of brambles. The king's wounds were not severe; however, his feet were injured the most. He had healed in several days with the exception of one foot, where a thorn had pierced deeply and festered.

The best doctors in the kingdom treated the wound with all their skill. They bathed, poulticed, and bandaged it, but all was in vain. The foot grew worse and became more swollen and painful. Finally, word was received of a wonderful doctor in a distant land who was a very successful healer. Unfortunately, he never left his home country; he expected his patients to come to him. The king offered a large sum of money to persuade the famous physician to travel to his kingdom.

When he arrived, the doctor examined the king's foot and told him that it was beyond the power of man to heal, but that he could deaden the pain so that the king could walk without suffering. The king was very grateful. The doctor told the king to have the royal shoemaker make a slipper of goatskin that was very loose and comfortable. In the meantime, the physician prepared a secret preparation to coat the slipper. Eight days later the physician appeared and brought the slipper in a case. He fitted it to the king's foot and over the slipper rubbed a polish whiter than snow.

The doctor told the king, "While you wear this slipper you will not feel the slightest pain because I have rubbed it inside and out with balsam, which has the quality of strengthening the material it touches. If your majesty were to live a thousand years, you would find this slipper as comfortable then as it is now."

The king tried out the new slipper and found that he could walk and run easily without pain. He thanked the doctor and asked how he could reward him; in fact, he offered to pay him well if he stayed in the kingdom. The doctor said that he would take only what he had been offered, and that he must return home where many sick people were waiting for him. King Balancin bestowed royal honors on the physician and provided an escort for his journey home.

Two years later the king decided to have a birthday celebration and asked the princess to plan the festivities. Diamantina was fond of the river, so she planned a day of sailing and rowing followed by an evening of music, dancing, plays, and fireworks. On his birthday, the king and the princess walked down to the river; they boarded a splendid barge from which they watched swimming races and diving competitions. The barge then transported them upriver to the site of the plays and concerts.

As the king was boarding the barge to return to the palace, the white slipper caught on a nail. When the king shook his foot to free it, the precious slipper came off and fell into the river. It happened so fast that no one but the king knew what had happened. Diamantina looked down the river and could see a white speck disappearing downstream. The king's pain returned and as he turned, he staggered and fell into the river. Everyone immediately jumped to the king's aid, and one of the strong swimmers hauled the king to the shore.

The princess had been terrified at seeing her father disappear below the surface of the water. It took the king three days to recover from the cold, shock, and pain. The princess ordered an extensive search for the white slipper, but the best divers were unable to find it. Apparently it had been carried out to sea by the current. Diamantina sent messengers in search of the doctor who had brought relief to her father. They were told that the doctor had died and that his secret had died with him.

The king's pain did not lessen, so he ordered another search of the riverbed, again without success. Finally, he issued a proclamation that whoever found the missing slipper would be made heir to the crown and could marry the princess. Diamantina's heart sank when she heard what her father had promised. Nevertheless, she loved her father so much and desired his comfort more than anything in the world, so she bowed her head and said nothing.

The riverbanks became crowded as the princess's suitors from distant lands joined the search. One local youth always lingered longer than the rest and searched during the night, even though his clothes stuck to his skin and his teeth chattered.

One day the king was lying in bed racked with pain when he heard the sound of a scuffle outside his chamber. He sent for a servant who said that a young man from the town had had the impudence to ask to measure the royal foot, so he could make a slipper to replace the lost one.

When the king asked what his servants had done with the young man, he was told that they had thrown him out of the palace and given him a few hard knocks. The king told them they had treated the young man unfairly, since he had come in kindness. They replied that he was only a good-for-nothing boy, probably a shoemaker's apprentice, and asked what good a new slipper would be without the soothing balsam. The king told them to bring the youth back all the same; he was willing to try anything that would relieve his pain.

The young man was tall and handsome and, although he said that he made shoes, his manners were pleasant and modest. He bowed low as he asked the king not only to allow him to measure the royal foot but also to apply a healing plaster on the wound.

King Balancin was pleased with the voice and appearance of the youth, who seemed to know what he was doing. The young man measured the foot and applied the plaster, which quickly soothed the pain.

The king asked the young man what his name was. He said that he was called Gilguerillo because, even though he had lost his parents when he was six, he went about town singing and generally was happy. The king asked him if he really thought that he could cure him; the youth said that he could do it in about two weeks. When asked if there was anything that he needed, the young man asked for a fast horse. The king told him that if he succeeded, he knew what his reward would be. However, if he failed, he would be flogged for his impudence.

Gilguerillo bowed and left the palace, followed by the jeers of the crowd. A magnificent horse was led up to him, which he mounted with agility. He rode out of town listening to the jests of the assembled crowd, who didn't think he would succeed.

Gilguerillo had lived for many years with his uncle, an apothecary who had spent his life studying chemistry. The uncle could leave no money to his nephew because he had a son of his own, but he taught him all that he knew. When his uncle died, Gilguerillo kept the apothecary's shop open.

On the morning before the birthday celebration when the princess had walked though town, Gilguerillo had seen her and had fallen hopelessly in love with her. He realized that a poor apothecary's nephew could never marry the king's daughter; however, the king's proclamation filled him with hope. He spent considerable time and effort in the river looking for the king's slipper until he realized that it would not be by the river that he would win the princess.

Gilguerillo turned to his books. He believed in the old proverb: "Everything comes to him who waits." One day he was reading a book of remedies hundreds of years old when he found a description of balsam—which could cure most kinds of sore or wound—distilled from a plant found only in a distant country. He verified that the king's foot could be cured by it and mounted his horse to travel there, which took six days.

Upon Gilguerillo's arrival, he searched for balsam on his hands and knees in a wooded area. He had difficulty finding any and at dusk, when he was about to give up for the day, he found a large bed of the plant. He picked every scrap that he could find and then mounted his horse to return home. He entered the town gates at night. His deadline was the next day. He was tired and his body ached but he kindled a fire, filled a pot with water, threw in the herbs, and let them boil. Then he slept soundly.

When Gilguerillo awoke, he checked the pot and found a thick syrup, just as the book had predicted. He lifted the syrup out with a spoon, spread it in the sun until it was partly dry, and poured it into a small flask. Then he washed thoroughly, put on his best clothes, put the flask in his pocket, and left for the palace, where he asked to see the king.

The king had been waiting anxiously for Gilguerillo's return, even though his foot was less painful since it had been wrapped in plaster. When Gilguerillo entered the king's chambers and the king didn't see a slipper, he thought that the young man had failed. Gilguerillo took the flask out of his pocket and poured a few drops on the wound. He told the king to repeat that for three nights, and he would be cured. Gilguerillo left quickly before the king could thank him. The townspeople continued to jeer him.

On the fourth morning, the king checked his foot, and it was completely healed. There wasn't even a scar. The king was over-joyed. He sent for his daughter and asked the young man to be brought to the palace. When she saw him, the princess saw that he was young and really handsome. She was thankful that it was not some dreadful old man who had cured her father. While the king was announcing to his courtiers the wonderful cure that had been made, Diamantina was thinking that if Gilguerillo looked so well in common clothes, how much better he would look in the splendid garments of a king's son. Nevertheless, she remained silent and watched with amusement as the courtiers paid homage and deferred to the apothecary's nephew.

The stewards brought Gilguerillo a magnificent tunic of green velvet bordered with gold and a cap with three plumes in it. When the princess saw him in his new finery, she fell in love with him immediately. The wedding was planned for the following week. At the ball, no one danced as long or as lively as King Balancin.

Moral: Resourcefulness and perseverance are two of the
        strongest human qualities.

Based on: Andrew Lang, "The White Slipper,"
        The Orange Fairy Book

The Legend of the Patient Suitor

Once there was a poor family with one son. One day the boy said to his mother, "Go to Toros Beg and ask for the hand of his daugh-ter for me. The mother answered, "My son, Toros Beg is the town's richest man, and we are the town's poorest people. How can you suggest that I ask for his daughter?" Her son told her just to go and ask. She hesitated, but he kept after her.

Finally she could not bear her son's unhappiness any longer and went to the rich man's house and said, "I am going to ask a great favor of you. I hope that you may see fit to grant it, although I am ashamed to ask such a thing."

"What is it that you want?" the man asked.

"My son wants to marry your daughter."

"All right," the rich man answered, "Tell your son to come and see me."

Amazed, the mother went home and told her son what the rich man had said, and the boy went to the rich man's house. The rich man said, "My boy, I will let you marry my daughter if you go to the village of Van and learn the story of the man who washes clothes from dawn to sunset and yet he cannot even finish washing a single handkerchief."

The boy went to Van where he saw a man by the brook about to wash a handkerchief that he held in his right hand. The man looked up at the steeple on a nearby church, ran up to it, looked about and ran back again. He did this from dawn to sunset and did not wash a single handkerchief.

Running alongside him, the boy asked, "Friend, why do you continually run up and down? Why don't you stay here and wash your handkerchief?"

"I cannot answer your question until you go to the village of Moush where you will find, in front of the church, a blind beggar. He asks for alms, but when people give him anything, he says, 'Take this away and slap me instead.' If you can discover why he does this, I will tell you my story," the washer said.

The boy left the washer and headed for the village of the blind beggar. He found the church and saw the blind man there, just as the washer had told him. Whenever someone took pity on him and gave him a few coins, he said, "Please take this back and slap my face instead."

After watching the blindman for a while, the boy asked him, "Why do you refuse to take alms and instead ask people to slap you? If you will tell me this, the washer at Van will tell me his secret and I can go back home and marry the girl of my choice."

"In the village of Erevan there is a very wealthy merchant. When he goes with his caravans, he is gone for six years and brings back many rare and precious things. Immediately upon his return, he goes to a place where he has set two huge rocks and knocks himself first against one and then against the other. If you can learn why he does this and then return to me, I will tell you my story," the blind beggar said.

Six years later the merchant returned with great riches from all parts of the world. He went to the site where he had placed the two rocks and knocked himself first against one rock and then against the other. He did this until he was bleeding and falling down in a faint. Then he was taken home, and healers anointed his bruised body.

The boy waited until the merchant was healed and went to him and asked, "You are a wealthy and successful man. Tell me, why do you knock yourself against those two rocks and hurt yourself? If you tell me this, the beggar in Moush will tell me his story and the washer in Van will tell me his story. Then I can go home and marry the girl of my choice. I have been waiting for your return for over six years."

"My son, if you had enough patience to wait for me six years, I will tell you the story of my life. When I was young I decided to seek my fortune. I left my pregnant wife and went away. I roamed the land, bought and traded, and after twenty years became a rich man and decided to return home. When I reached my village, I peeked into a window of my house to see if anyone was home and saw my wife lying beside a handsome youth.

Thinking that she had been unfaithful to me, I took my bow and arrow and shot both my wife and the man. Then I went and slept at the tavern. The next morning I heard that someone had killed my wife and my young son. If I had more patience, this would not have happened. Now I must repent, and that is why I knock myself against those two rocks to punish myself," the merchant told him.

The boy thanked him and said, "Now I can go back to the beggar, and he will tell me his story." The boy returned to the church where the blind man was begging. "I have seen the merchant, and he has told me his story. Now, will you tell me yours?" the boy asked.

The blind man asked what he had been told, and the boy told him the story of the penitent merchant. "Now tell me your story," he asked, "So I can return to the washer to hear his story. Then I can return home and marry Toros Beg's daughter."

The blind man told the boy his story. At one time he had been a camel driver and transported loads from one village to another. One day a dervish came to him and told him that he had a load to be taken to Kharput. The dervish said that he would load forty camels with gold. If the camel driver would take thirty-nine of them to Kharput, he could have one of them.

The dervish asked him if he agreed with this and he said that did. He and the dervish entered a cave where the dervish took a small box off the shelf and put it in his pocket. They loaded the camels with gold and left.

The camel driver thought how much better it would be if he had ten camels instead of one, so he told the dervish that he wouldn't transport his load unless he gave him nine more camels loaded with gold. The dervish gave him nine more camels. A little further down the road, he told the dervish that he wanted another ten camels. Even further down the road he told the dervish that he wanted ten more camels to make his total thirty. The dervish agreed. Finally, he told the dervish that he wanted all forty camels. Again, surprisingly, the dervish agreed.

Still the camel driver was not satisfied. He remembered the little box that the dervish had put into his pocket. He wondered what was in the box. It might be something more valuable than gold. He asked the dervish about it and was told that it contained magic for dervishes like him. He demanded that the dervish give him the box.

The dervish told the camel driver, "In this box there is a medicine. If it is applied to one eye, it enables a person to see what is beneath this earth of ours, such as the location of oil deposits and buried treasure. But if the medicine is applied to both eyes, the person will become blind. Here, since you insist, take the box, but be careful how you use it."

The camel driver took the medicine and applied it to one of his eyes, and he could see oil deposits and treasure buried beneath the earth. He still wasn't satisfied. He reasoned that if he could see those things with the medicine on one eye, he should be able to see even more if he applied the medicine to both eyes.

So he put the medicine on the other eye and became blind, as the dervish told him he would. He called out to the dervish to help him and was told, "You are too selfish ever to enjoy life. Therefore remain as you are and repent." The dervish slapped his face and left with all forty camels and the box. The camel driver told the boy that was his story.

The boy thanked him and told him that now he would go to the washer and hear his tale. He told the washer that he had heard the stories of the blind man and the merchant and asked to hear his story. The washer asked to be told the blindman's story first, and then he told his.

"Many years ago I was a poor washerman on this road, and I

washed clothes for passersby. One day when I returned to my hut, I saw that it was not a hut any longer but a beautiful palace. The door opened, and I was surprised to see a beautiful women, like an angel, standing before me. She said, 'Come in, this is your home, and this is your family.' She took me into a room that was filled with precious gems. The curtains and rugs were made of pure silk, and the throne in the center of the room was magnificent. In the room were thirty-nine other women just as beautiful as the one who had opened the door for me."

"We are all here to live with you. You can eat and sleep with any one of us. But here is one condition. You must never express dissatisfaction. If you do so three times, you will be just as poor as you ever were," the most beautiful of the women said.

"So I stayed with them and ate and slept with them. In fact, one of them even bore me a child. Everything was plentiful, and I led an easy life. One day, however, it was very misty, and I said, 'Why is it so misty today? Why isn't the weather pleasant sometimes?'" The most beautiful woman reminded me that I had complained once, and that I only had two more chances to complain left. Several months went by until one day, when it was very rainy, I said, 'Is there a hole in the sky? Why is it so rainy?'" The leader of the beautiful women reminded me to be careful because I had now had complained twice and would lose the palace if I complained again.

"Months passed until one day it was very hot. It was so hot I was having difficulty breathing, so I said, 'What a hot day! I can scarcely breathe!' No sooner had I said this than everything had disappeared, and I found myself in my old broken-down hut. Now, when I begin to do the washing, I look up to the steeple and see my wife and child. But when I run up to speak to them they are gone. That is why I cannot even wash a handkerchief from dawn to sunset," the washer explained.

The boy thanked the washer and said, "Now I can return home and marry Toros Beg's daughter." When he returned to the rich man, he told each of these stories that he had spent years to hear.

"My son, since you showed such patience in learning these stories, you are the right man to marry my daughter." And so the boy married the beautiful girl and they lived happily.

Moral: Patience is a strong virtue in short supply. Greed, which is not a virtue, frequently is followed by repentance.

Based on: Susie Hoogasian-Villa, "The Patient Suitor,"
100 Armenian Tales

Chapter 5

INDEFATIGABLE / UNSELFISH

High though his titles, proud though his name,
Boundless his wealth as wish can claim,
Despite those titles, power, and pelf,
The wretch concentered all in self,
Living, shall forfeit fair renown,
And doubly dying, shall go down
To the vile dust from whence he sprung,
Unwept, unhonored, and unsung.

Sir Walter Scott, *Lay of the Last Minstrel*

The Legend of the Four Gifts

In Brittany there lived a woman named Barbaik Bourhis, who spent all her days working on her farm with the help of her niece Tephany. Early and late in the day they could be seen in the fields or in the dairy, milking cows and making butter, or feeding the ducks and chickens.

Perhaps Barbaik would have been better off if she had allowed herself time to rest and to think of other things; she began to love money for its own sake. She allowed herself and Tephany only the food and clothing that they absolutely needed. She hated poor people and thought that such lazy creatures had no business in the world.

Barbaik was beside herself with anger one day when she found Tephany outside the cowbarn talking to young Dennis, a poor day laborer from the village of Plover. Taking her niece by the arm, she pulled her briskly away, exclaiming, "Are you not ashamed, girl, to waste your time on a man who is poor as a mouse, when there are a dozen more who would be only too happy to buy you rings of silver, if you would let them?" Tephany told her aunt that Dennis was a good workman, as she herself knew, and that he had saved his money and soon would be able to buy a farm.

"Nonsense," cried Barbaik. "He will never save enough for a farm until he is a hundred. I would rather see you in your grave than the wife of a man whose whole fortune is the shirt on his back."

Tephany asked her aunt what fortune matters when one is young and strong.

"What does fortune matter?" retorted Barbaik. "Is it possible that you are really so foolish as to despise money? If this is what you learn from Dennis, I forbid you to talk with him, and I will send him away if he shows up here again. Now go and wash the clothes and spread them out to dry."

With a heavy heart, Tephany went down to the river. "She is harder than these rocks," the girl said to herself. "Yes, a thousand times harder. For the rain can at last wear down the stone, but I might cry forever, and she would never care. Talking to Dennis is the only pleasure I have, and if I am cannot see him, I might as well enter a convent."

Thinking these thoughts, Tephany reached the riverbank and unfolded the large bundle of linen to be washed. The tap of a stick made her look up. Standing beside her was a little old woman, a stranger. Tephany asked the woman if she would like to sit down and rest. In a trembling voice the old woman told her that when the sky is the only roof you have, you rest where you can.

Tephany asked her if she had any friends who would welcome her into their homes. The old woman replied that all her friends had died, and that the only friends she had were strangers with kind hearts.

Tephany hesitated and then offered a small loaf of bread and some bacon intended for her dinner. She added that at least today the old woman would eat well.

Gazing at Tephany, the woman said that those who help others deserve to be helped themselves. She knew that Tephany's eyes were red because Barbaik had forbidden her to speak to the young man from Plover. She told Tephany to cheer up because she was a good girl. The old woman promised to give Tephany something to enable her to see Dennis once every day. Tephany was astounded to learn that the woman knew about her affairs.

The old woman told Tephany, "Take this long copper pin and every time you stick it in your dress, your aunt will be obliged to leave the house to go and count her cabbages. As long as the pin is in your dress you will be free, and your aunt will not return until you have placed the pin back in its case." The woman got up, nodded to Tephany, and vanished.

Tephany stood on the riverbank, still as a stone. If it had not been for the pin in her hands, she would have thought that she had been dreaming. She knew that it had not been a ordinary woman who had given her the pin, but a fairy. Suddenly, Tephany's eyes fell upon the clothes, and to make up for lost time she began to scrub them vigorously.

The next evening, at the time when Dennis usually waited for her in the shadow of the cowbarn, Tephany stuck the pin in her dress. Immediately, Barbaik put on her wooden shoes and walked through the orchard to the cabbage patch in the fields. The girl ran from the house and spent an enjoyable hour with Dennis. This scene was repeated for many evenings. Eventually, though, Tephany began to notice a change that made her sad.

At first Dennis seemed to enjoy their time together as much as she did; however, when he had taught her all the songs he knew, and had told her all his plans for growing rich and becoming a great man, he did not have much to say to her. Like many people, he was fond of talking about himself but not of listening to anyone else. Occasionally, he wouldn't come to visit her and instead would tell her that he had business in town. She didn't reproach him, but she was not deceived. She realized that he no longer cared for her as he used to.

Day by day Tephany's heart grew heavier and her cheeks paler. One evening after she had waited for Dennis in vain, she went down to the spring to fill the water pot. The fairy who had given her the pin stood in the path in front of her.

The old woman observed that Tephany hardly looked happier than before, even though she could see her lover now whenever she wanted to.

Tephany told the fairy how Dennis had tired of her, and how he made excuses to stay away. She said that it wasn't enough to see him, but that she must be able to amuse him. Concluding that Dennis was clever, she asked the fairy to help her to be clever too.

The old woman asked her if that was what she really wanted. When Tephany insisted that it was, the fairy gave her a feather to stick in her hair. She told Tephany that it would make her as wise as Solomon.

After thanking the old woman, Tephany went home and stuck the feather into the ribbon that she always wore in her hair. Soon she heard Dennis coming and, since her aunt was counting cabbages, she ran out to greet him.

The young man was amazed by Tephany's conversation. There seemed to be nothing that she did not know. She could sing songs from every part of Brittany and could even compose songs herself. Dennis wondered if this was really the quiet girl who had been so anxious to learn all that he could teach her, or whether it was actually someone else.

Night after night, Dennis came back and found Tephany growing wiser and wiser. Soon the neighbors expressed their surprise as well. When they heard her jests, though, they considered her ill-natured. They said that the man who married her would find that she was the one who held the reins and drove the cart. Dennis began to agree with them. Since he liked to be the master, he became concerned about Tephany's sharp tongue. Instead of laughing when she made fun of people, he was uncomfortable, thinking that his turn would come next.

One evening Dennis told Tephany that he couldn't stay because he had promised to go to a dance in the next village. She was disappointed; she had worked hard all day and was looking forward to spending some time with him. She tried to persuade him to stay with her but he refused.

She became angry and told him that she knew why he didn't want to miss the dance: because Alice of Penenru would be there. Alice was the loveliest girl for miles around, and she and Dennis had known each other since childhood. Dennis admitted that Alice would be at the dance, and that it was worth going a long way to watch her dance.

Angrily, Tephany told Dennis to go. She ran into the house, slamming the door behind her. She was lonely and miserable as she sat down by the fire and stared into the embers. She flung the feather from her hair and, put her head in her hands, and sobbed bitterly. She wondered what was the use of being clever when it was beauty that men wanted. She thought to herself that it was too late; Dennis would never come back.

Suddenly, she heard a voice at her side and saw the old woman leaning on her stick. Since Tephany wanted beauty so much, the woman gave her a necklace to wear around her neck. The fairy told her that as long as she wore it, she would be the most beautiful woman in the region.

Tephany thanked the fairy and joyfully took the necklace, put it on, and fastened the clasp. She looked in the mirror and realized that she would no longer fear competition from Alice or any other girl, for surely none were as fair as she. She put on her best dress and shoes and hurried to the dance. Along the way she encountered a beautiful carriage with a young lord seated in it. He saw how beautiful Tephany was and told her that no young women in his region could compare with her. He immediately decided that she would be his bride.

The carriage was large and blocked the narrow road, so Tephany was forced, against her will, to remain where she was. She begged the young lord to go on his way, while she went hers. She told him that she was only a poor peasant girl used to milking cows and spinning yarn. He told her that she might be a peasant, but that he would make her a great lady. He took her hand and tried to lead her to the carriage.

Tephany told him that she didn't want to be a great lady; she just wanted to be the wife of Dennis. She threw off his hand and tried to hide in the ditch, but the young man's attendants seized her and put her in the coach, closed the door, and told the coachman to drive on.

An hour later, they arrived at a splendid castle, and Tephany was lifted out of the carriage and carried into the hall, while a priest was sent for to perform the wedding ceremony. The young man told her about all the beautiful things she would have as his wife.

Tephany didn't listen to him; she looked around for a way to escape. Three great doors were barred; however, the door through which she had entered was shut with a spring, and she could see an opening between the door and its frame. Touching the copper pin in her dress, she sent everyone in the hall out to count cabbages. Then she ran through the door that she had come in. She wandered around not knowing where she was going but continued down the road until she heard a dog barking at a farm.

The farmer's wife and sons were standing in front of the house. When the mother heard Tephany's request for a bed for the night, the good wife's heart softened and she was going to invite her inside; unfortunately, her sons, who were impressed by Tephany's beauty, began to quarrel as to who could do the most for her. The words led to blows among the young men, and suddenly, Tephany was no longer welcome there.

Tephany ran down the nearest path, but she could hear footsteps behind her. She took off the necklace and placed it around the neck of pig that was grunting in a nearby ditch. Now that her charm had vanished, she heard the footsteps turn from pursuing her to chasing the pig. She ran on until she arrived at her aunt's house.

For several days Tephany was so tired and unhappy that she could barely finish her work. To make matters worse, Dennis rarely came to visit. She grew paler and paler, until everyone noticed it except her aunt. The water pot was too heavy for her now, but she continued to make her trips to the spring.

Tephany wondered how she could have been so foolish as to ask for what she had requested. She should not have asked for the freedom to see Dennis, or a quick tongue, or beauty. She realized that she should have asked the fairy for riches to make life easy for herself and others.

Not surprisingly, the fairy appeared on the spot to respond to Tephany's most recent desire. The old woman told Tephany to look in her right-hand pocket when she arrived home and she would find a small box. If she would rub her eyes with the ointment in the box, she would find a priceless treasure.

Tephany ran back to the farm as quickly as she could and took the small box out of her pocket. She was rubbing her eyes with the ointment when her aunt entered the room. Barbaik asked her niece what she was doing and demanded to know why she was not out in the fields working. Barbaik had been working hard all day and asked Tephany if she wasn't ashamed to let the farm go to ruin. Tephany tried to defend herself, but her aunt was really angry and boxed her ears.

At this, Tephany could no longer control herself. She burst into tears. To her surprise, she saw that each teardrop was a round and shining pearl. Barbaik went down on her knees to pick them up from the floor. She was still gathering them up when Dennis entered the house. He asked if the tears were really pearls and fell on his knees also. He looked up and saw more pearls rolling down Tephany's cheeks. Barbaik told Dennis that he could have his share, but that they should make sure that the neighbors heard nothing about it.

Tephany could not bear any more. She was choked up by their greed and turned to run from the room. Barbaik caught her by the arm and said many tender words to make her cry more. Tephany finally wiped her eyes, but her aunt asked if Tephany could cry more pearls. Barbaik then asked Dennis if he thought if would help if they beat her a little. At that, Dennis shook his head.

Barbaik and Dennis decided that they had gathered enough pearls for the first time and went into town to find out the value of each pearl. Tephany sat quietly in her chair, her hands clasped tightly, as if she were forcing something back. At last she raised her eyes and saw the fairy standing by the hearth, with a mocking look in her eyes.

Tephany trembled. She jumped up and handed the pin, the feather, and the box to the old woman. Tephany cried out, "Here they are, all of them. They belong to you. Let me never see them again, but I have learned the lesson that they have taught me. Others may have wit, beauty, and riches, but for me I desire noth-. ing but to be the poor peasant girl I always was, working hard for those she loves."

The fairy said that Tephany had learned her lesson, and promised that now the young woman would lead a peaceful life and marry the man she loved. The fairy reminded Tephany that everything she had done was for Dennis, not for herself.

Tephany never saw the old woman again, and she forgave Dennis for selling her tears. In time, he grew to be a good husband, who did his share of the work.

Moral: Be careful what you wish for; you might get it. Also, greed, though common, is one the least desirable human traits.

Based on: Andrew Lang, "The Four Gifts," *The Lilac Fairy Book*

The Legend of the Stonecutter

Once there lived a stonecutter who went every day to a great rock in the side of a large mountain and cut slabs of stone for houses and for gravestones. He knew his trade well and was a careful workman with many customers. For a long while he was happy with his lot and wanted nothing better.

A spirit who lived in the mountain occasionally appeared to men and helped them to become rich. The stonecutter had never seen the spirit and shook his head in disbelief whenever anyone mentioned it.

One day the stonecutter carried a gravestone to the house of a prosperous man and saw there many beautiful things of which he had never dreamed. Suddenly his daily work seemed to grow harder and heavier, and he said to himself that he wished he were a rich man so he could sleep in a bed with silk curtains and gold tassels. He thought about how happy that would make him. A voice answered him that his wish had been heard and that he would become a rich man.

The stonecutter looked around at the sound of the voice but could see no one. He thought that it must have been his imagination. He picked up his tools and went home; he did not feel like working any more that day. When he reached the site of his little house, he stood and stared in awe. Instead of his wooden hut, there was a stately palace filled with splendid furniture, including a bed like the one that he had envied. He was beside himself with joy. His old life was soon forgotten.

In early summer, the sun blazed fiercely. One morning the stonecutter could scarcely breathe so he returned home early. He looked through the window blinds into the street and saw a carriage pass by that was drawn by servants dressed in blue and silver. An umbrella was held over the head of the prince sitting in the carriage to protect him from the sun's rays. As the carriage vanished around the corner, the stonecutter said, "If only I were a prince and could travel in such a carriage and have a golden umbrella held over my head, how happy I would be."

The voice of the mountain spirit answered that the stonecutter's wish had been granted, and that he was now a prince. One company of men rode before his carriage, and another rode behind it. He was attended by servants dressed in scarlet and gold, an umbrella was held over his head, and everything that his heart could desire was his.

But it was not enough; he looked around for something to wish for. Then he saw that, although his grass had been watered, the sun scorched it. Also, despite the umbrella held over his head each day, his face grew browner and browner. He cried out, "The sun is mightier than I; oh, if I were only the sun!"

The mountain spirit answered that his wish had been granted, and that he was now the sun. The stonecutter was proud of his power. He directed his beams above and below, on earth and in heaven. He burned the grass in the fields and scorched the faces of princes as well as poor people. However, before long he tired of his might because it seemed there was nothing left for him to do. Discontent filled his soul. When a cloud covered his face and hid the earth from him, he cried out in anger that the cloud was holding his rays captive. The sun wondered if the cloud was mightier that he. He exclaimed that if he were a cloud, he would be mightier than anyone.

The mountain spirit told him that his wish had been granted, and that he was now a cloud. He was positioned between the sun and the earth; he caught the sun's beams and held them. To his joy the earth grew green again, and the flowers blossomed. But the cloud could not prevent the rain from pouring forth until rivers overflowed and crops stood in fields of water. Towns and villages were inundated by rain, and only the great rock on the side of the mountain was unmoved. The cloud was amazed to see this and wondered if the rock was mightier than he. He wished that he were the rock.

The mountain spirit told the stonecutter that his wish had been heard, and that he was now the rock. The rock stood proudly and neither the heat of the sun nor the force of the rain could move him. He considered this the best so far. One day, however, he heard a strange noise at his feet.

He looked down and saw a stonecutter driving tools into his surface. A great chunk of the rock fell to the ground, and he felt a trembling run all through him. In his wrath, he cried out, wondering if a mere child of the earth was mightier than the earth. He wished that he were a man again.

Again, the mountain spirit answered that his wish had been granted, and that he was a man again. By the sweat of his brow, the stonecutter again toiled at his trade. His bed was hard and he didn't have much food, but he had learned to be satisfied. He did not long to be someone or something else. Since he never asked for what he didn't have or desired to be greater or mightier than others, he was happy at last. He no longer heard the voice of the mountain spirit.

Moral: Be careful what you ask for; you might get it. Sometimes
     we should be satisfied with what we have.

Based on: Andrew Lang, "The Stonecutter,"
     The Crimson Fairy Book

How to Find a True Friend

Once upon a time there lived a king and queen who longed to have a son. They made a vow at the shrine of St. James that if their prayers were answered, the boy would set out on a pilgrimage at the age of eighteen. Their wish was granted and they had a son. Everyone said he was the most beautiful baby they had ever seen.

The boy grew bigger and stronger every day. The king died when the boy was twelve years old, leaving the prince to take care of his mother.

Six years passed, and the boy's eighteenth birthday approached. When the queen thought about this, her heart sank, for her son was the light of her life. How could she send him forth into the unknown dangers that a pilgrim encounters? Daily she grew more and more sorrowful and wept bitterly when she was alone. She thought that no one else knew how sad she was until her son asked why she cried all day long.

The queen told her son that only one thing in the world troubled her. He asked if she thought that her property was being badly managed and offered to look into the matter. He rode off into the country where his mother owned great estates. Everything was in order, and the prince rode home to report to her. He told her that she could be happy again. Her estates were better managed than anyone else's, her cattle were thriving, and the fields are thick with corn, ripe for the harvest.

Although the queen told her son that was good news, it didn't seem to make any difference to her. The next morning she was weeping and wailing as loudly as ever. The prince begged her to tell him the cause of her tears. At that, he told him about the vow made before he was born that he would make a pilgrimage to St. James's shrine when he was eighteen. It was the thought of being parted from him that caused her grief. Since the shrine was far away, he would be gone for over a year.

The queen was sad that she would not see her son for such a long time. The prince assured his mother that he would return to her. He told her that as long as he was alive, he would return home. On his eighteenth birthday he mounted his best horse and said good-bye to the queen. He promised her that with the help of fate, he would return as soon as he could.

The queen burst into tears. Before her son left, she took three apples from her pocket and handed them to him. She said that he would need a good companion on his long journey. She told him that if he encountered a young man whom he would like to accompany him, to invite him to an inn to have dinner. After dinner, he should cut one of the apples into unequal parts and ask his potential friend to take one. "If he takes the larger part," she warned, "leave him, for he is not a true friend. However, if he takes the smaller part, treat him as your brother and share with him all you have." The queen kissed her son again, blessed him, and let him go.

The prince traveled a long way without seeing anybody on the road. Finally he caught up with a youth about his own age. When the stranger asked him where he was going, the prince replied that he was making a pilgrimage to the shrine of St. James to fulfill a vow. The stranger said that he was going to the shrine also and suggested that they travel together. The prince held off getting on familiar terms with the stranger until he had tested him with the apple.

When they reached an inn, the prince said that he was hungry and suggested they stop for a meal. After dinner, the prince pulled out an apple from his pocket and cut it into a big half and a small half. He offered both to the stranger, who took the larger half. The prince thought to himself that this was no friend of his. In order to part company, the prince pretended to be ill and unable to travel that day. The stranger said that he was in a hurry and decided to push on.

The prince remained at the inn for a while to allow the other young man a good head start. Afterwards the prince rode alone for a distance, but the way seemed long and dull by himself. He was a sociable person and hoped to meet a true friend for a travel companion. Soon he caught up with another young man who asked where the prince was going. The prince told him the object of his journey. Coincidentally, the young man was fulfilling a similar vow. They decided to ride together, and the road seemed shorter to the prince now that he had company.

They reached an inn and the prince suggested that they stop for dinner. When they had finished eating, the prince took another apple from his pocket, cut it into unequal parts, and offered them to his companion, who immediately took the larger piece. The prince realized that again this was no friend of his. Once more, the prince pretended to be ill. When he had given the other youth enough of a head start, the prince continued on. He was even more bored than before and wished for a companion.

Finally the prince saw another young man ahead and caught up with him. The young man asked the prince where he was going and was told that his destination was the shrine of St. James. The young man said that he was going there, too, and the prince suggested that they travel together. The miles seemed to fly by. The prince hoped that this young man would prove to be a true friend, because he was lively and entertaining.

Soon they came to an inn, and the prince suggested that they stop to eat. After dinner, the prince drew the last apple out of his pocket and cut it into a big part and a small part. This time, the young man took the smaller piece, and the prince was glad that he had at last found a true friend. The prince told the young man that they would be brothers, and that he would share with him all he had. They agreed to travel together to the shrine. If one of them died along the way, the other would carry his body there.

It took the young men an entire year to reach the shrine, and they passed through many lands on their way. One day they arrived tired and half-starved in a large city. They rented a small house near the royal castle to rest for a while. The following morning, the king of the country stepped out on his balcony and saw the two young men in the garden of the house next door. He thought to himself that they were handsome youths, but one was more handsome than the other. In fact, the prince was more handsome than his friend. On the spur of the moment, the king decided that his daughter should marry the prince.

The king asked the young men to dinner and received them with the utmost kindness when they arrived at the castle. He introduced the prince to his daughter who was lovely beyond words. At bedtime, the king arranged for the other young man to be given a poisoned drink, which killed him in a few minutes. The king reasoned that if his friend died, the prince would call off his pilgrimage and stay there and marry the princess.

When the prince awoke the next morning, he looked for his friend. The king reported that the young man had died during the night and was to be buried immediately. The prince told his host that if his friend had died, he could stay no longer in the castle but must continue his journey. The king tried to convince him to stay and marry his daughter. The prince insisted that he must continue on. He asked for a good horse and promised to return and marry the princess after he had fulfilled his parents' vow.

The prince mounted the horse, placed his dear friend's body in front of him on the saddle, and rode away. The young man was not really dead, just in a deep sleep. When the prince reached the shrine of St. James, he dismounted from his horse, cradled his friend in his arms as if he were a child, and placed him before the altar. The prince said, "St. James, I have fulfilled the vow my parents made for me. I have come myself to your shrine and have brought my friend. I place him in your hands. Restore him to life, I pray, for although he is dead, he has fulfilled his vow also." Before the prince had finished his prayer, his friend got up and stood before him, as well as ever. The young men gave their thanks and headed for home.

When they arrived back in the king's city, they stayed in the small house by the castle. Rejoicing that the prince had kept his word and returned, the king ordered great feasts to be prepared and the wedding of his daughter to the prince to be planned for the following week. The prince himself could imagine no greater good fortune. After they were married, the young couple lived happily at the castle.

After a few months, the prince reminded the king that his mother was anxiously waiting for him. He told his father-in-law that he was going to take his wife and friend and start for home. The king acknowledged the prince's obligations and gave orders to make the necessary preparations for the journey.

In his heart the king disliked the youth he had tried to kill. In order to separate him from the prince, he ordered the young man to deliver a message to a distant place. He told him to hurry and that the prince would delay his departure until he returned. As soon as the friend had left, the king went into the prince's chamber and told him that unless he started immediately, he would not reach the place where they must camp for the night. The prince said that he could not leave without his friend. The king assured him that his friend would be back in a hour and that the king would give him his best horse to catch up with the prince.

The prince allowed himself to be persuaded and left with his wife on the journey home. Meanwhile the poor friend had not been able to deliver his message in the short time estimated by the king. When the young man arrived back at the castle, the king told him that the prince was a long way off by now, and that he should hurry to catch up with him. The young man bowed, left the castle, and followed the prince on foot; the king had not provided him with the promised horse. He ran night and day until he at last reached the place where the prince and his wife were camped. He sank down, a miserable object, worn out, and covered with mud and dust. The prince welcomed him with joyfully and tended him as he would a brother.

At last the prince arrived home. The queen had been watching and waiting in the palace the entire time her son had been away. She was overjoyed to see her son again and to meet her new daughter-in-law. She ordered a bed to be made for the sick friend and sent for the best doctors in the country. None of them could cure him, however.

After all the doctors had tried and failed, the queen was told that a strange old man had just knocked at the palace gate and said that he could cure the dying youth. He was a holy man who had heard of the trouble that the prince's friend was in and had come to help.

At this time, a baby daughter was born to the princess and the prince. The prince was very happy to have the child, but he was distracted by his dying friend. He was bending over the sickbed of his friend when the holy man entered the room. The holy man asked the prince if he wished his friend to be cured, and the prince said, "certainly." The holy man asked him what price he would be willing to pay. The prince said only to tell him what to do to heal him.

The old man told the prince that he must take his newborn child, open her veins, and smear the body of his friend with her blood. The prince was appalled at being asked to put the life of his daughter at risk. The holy man said that if the prince would do this his friend would be cured immediately. The prince cried with horror, for he loved the baby dearly. The holy man told the prince again that the only way he could save his friend was by risking his daughter's life.

After dusk the prince took the baby, opened her veins, and smeared her blood over the wounds of the sick man. The look of death immediately left the friend, and he grew strong and healthy once more. The baby girl lay as white and still as if she were dead, though. They placed her in the cradle and wept bitterly, because they thought that by morning she would be lost to them.

At sunrise the holy man returned and inquired about the health of the sick man. He was told that the young man was completely recovered. Then he asked where the baby was. The prince sadly replied that he thought she was dead. The holy man told him to check again, and a smiling baby looked up at them.

The old man said, "I am St. James of Lizia and have come to help you, for I have seen that you are a true friend. From here on, live happily, all of you, together, and if you have troubles, send for me and I will help you get through them." With these words he lifted his hand in blessing and vanished.

They obeyed him and were happy and contented, and they tried to make the people of the land happy and contented, too.

Moral: Loyalty and unselfishness are important human qualities.

Based on: Andrew Lang, "How to Find a True Friend,"
  The Crimson Fairy Book

The Legend of the Test

Once there was a beggar who sat at the foot of a bridge and asked for alms from passersby. Every day a rich young merchant stopped to throw him a few coins. One day the merchant had a shipment larger than usual, and he did not have enough money to pay the caravan owners. As he went to borrow the necessary funds from a friend, he was preoccupied. He passed the bridge but forgot to give a few coins to the beggar.

The beggar saw the young man pass him by. He was surprised that the merchant had not given him money and wondered if anything was wrong. He shouted for the young man to come back. When the merchant returned, the beggar asked him why he had forgotten to give him money.

The young man replied that he was in a hurry and had just forgotten. He threw a few coins to the beggar. The beggar told him that he didn't want his money; he just wanted to know why he had forgotten and what was the matter.

The merchant told the beggar that he was hurrying to get money from a friend to pay a caravan owner. The beggar asked him how much he needed, and the merchant named the amount. The beggar told him to come to his house after dark, and he would give him what he needed. The young man protested that the beggar had nothing. "Come to my house," the beggar repeated, "and you will get your money.'

That night the merchant went to the beggar's house. To his amazement, he found that it was larger than the homes of his rich friends. A charming girl invited him in and made him comfortable. After she had served him Turkish coffee, the beggar came into the room, greeted him, and asked his daughter to bring the money bag to him. They counted out the money that the merchant needed. The beggar told him that he could return the loan whenever he had the money. There was no hurry.

The merchant thanked them and went home. At home he began thinking of the loveliness and grace of the beggar's daughter and realized that he had fallen in love with her. Several days later when the merchant returned the money, he asked the beggar if he could marry his daughter. The beggar asked the young man if he had a trade. The young man replied that being a merchant was the only kind of work that he knew.

The beggar told the merchant that he would give him the hand of his daughter on one condition. The merchant would have to wear the beggar's clothes and sit at the foot of the bridge begging for one day. The beggar told him that if he would do that, he could marry his daughter.

The next morning, in tattered clothes, the merchant sat at the foot of the bridge and begged alms from passersby. They recognized him and knew that he had once been a rich man. Everyone felt pity for him and threw him money. The merchant was bitterly embarrassed, but what else could he do? He was willing to sacrifice his pride to marry the beggar's daughter.

That evening the merchant went to the beggar's house and placed the alms money on the table. The beggar acknowledged that the young man had satisfied the condition, and he passed the money back across the table to him. The beggar added that he didn't want the money; he just wanted to test the merchant to see how much he loved his daughter.

Now the beggar knew that if merchant's business ever failed, he could beg to support his wife. The young merchant and the beggar's daughter were married and lived happily.

Moral: Overcoming pride, one of the most common human
weaknesses, makes us better people.

Based on: Susie Hoogasian-Villa, "The Test,"
100 Armenian Tales

The Legend of the Enchanted Ring

Once there lived a young man named Rosimond, who was as good
and handsome as his elder brother Bramintho was ugly and wicked.
Their mother detested her older son and had eyes only for the
younger one. This made Bramintho jealous, so he invented a horrible story to ruin his brother. He told his father that Rosimond regularly visited a neighbor who was an enemy of the family, and that
he told him all that went on in their house, and, furthermore, that
Rosimond was plotting with the neighbor to poison his father.

The father flew into a rage and flogged Rosimond until he bled.
His father had him thrown into prison for three days without food.
Then he turned him out of the house and threatened to kill him if
he ever came back. His mother was miserable and wept bitterly, but
she dared not say anything.

Rosimond left home with tears in his eyes and no idea of where
to go. He wandered about for hours until he came to a thick wood.
Night fell as he reached a great rock, where he lay down and fell
asleep on a bed of moss, lulled by the music of a small brook. He
woke at dawn and saw before him a beautiful woman on a gray
horse with trappings of gold. She looked as if she were prepared for
the hunt. She asked him if he had seen a stag and a pack of hounds
pass by. He replied that he hadn't.

The horsewoman observed that Rosimond looked unhappy and
asked if anything was the matter. She gave him a diamond ring,
which she told him would make him the happiest and most powerful of men, provided that he didn't misuse it. She instructed him
that if he turned the diamond inside, he would become invisible. If
he turned the diamond outside, he would become visible again. If
he placed the ring on his little finger, he would take the shape of the
king's son, followed by a splendid court. If he placed it on his
fourth finger, he would take his own shape. The young man then
realized that it was a fairy who had spoken to him.

Rosimond was impatient to try the ring, and he returned home immediately. He found that the fairy had told him the truth; he could see and hear everything, while he was unseen. If he chose, he could take revenge on his brother without the slightest danger to himself. He told no one but his mother of the strange things that had befallen him. He put the enchanted ring on his little finger and appeared as the king's son, followed by a hundred fine horses and a guard of richly dressed officers.

Rosimond's father was surprised to see the King's son at his quiet little house, and he was embarrassed, not knowing the proper way to behave on such an occasion. Rosimond asked him how many sons he had. "Two," the father answered uneasily.

Rosimond asked his father to send for the sons, claiming that he would like to take them to court to make their fortunes. The father presented Bramintho to the supposed prince, who asked where the younger son was. He was told that the younger son had to be punished for misbehaving and had run away.

Rosimond told his father that he should have shown his younger son what was right, rather than punishing him. The prince took Bramintho with him to the palace and told his father that two guards would take him to a special place. The two guards took the father into the forest, where the fairy beat him with a birch rod. Then they cast him into a very deep and dark cave, where he lay enchanted. The fairy commanded him to stay there until his son came to free him.

Rosimond went to the King's palace while the real prince was away. The prince had sailed off to make war on a distant island; unfortunately, the winds had been contrary, and he was ship-wrecked and captured by a savage people. Rosimond appeared at the palace in the guise of the prince and told everyone that he had been rescued at the point of death by some merchants. His return triggered great public rejoicing, and the king could do nothing but embrace his son. The queen was even more moved, and celebrations were ordered across the kingdom.

One day the false prince told Bramintho that he had brought him to the palace to make his fortune, but hat he had found out that he had been a liar and was the cause of all the troubles of his brother Rosimond. The prince told Bramintho that he wanted him to speak to Rosimond and to listen to his reproaches. Bramintho trembled at this and admitted his deceit to the prince. The prince said that he wanted Bramintho to confess to his brother and to ask forgiveness.

Bramintho was filled with shame as soon as he saw Rosimond's face and begged his pardon, promising to atone for his past misdeeds. Rosimond embraced him tearfully and told his brother that he forgave him. He reminded Bramintho that he could have him sent to prison, but that he wanted to be as good to Bramintho as Bramintho had been deceitful to him.

Just then a furious war broke out between the king and the sovereign of the adjoining country, a bad man who never kept his word. Rosimond went to the palace of the wicked sovereign and, using the power of the ring, spied on his councils and learned his plans. Rosimond returned to his home country and took command of the army. He defeated the neighboring sovereign in battle and installed a peace with conditions that were universally just.

The king planned to marry his son to a lovely princess who was the heiress to a nearby kingdom. One morning Rosimond was hunting in the forest when his benefactress, the fairy, appeared before him. She cautioned him not to consider marrying someone who believed him to be a prince, and that he must never deceive anyone. She reminded him that the real prince, who the entire country thought Rosimond was, would have to succeed his father, for that was right and just.

The fairy told Rosimond to find the real prince on the distant island and bring him home to his family and his responsibilities. She told him to render this service to his master, the king, even though it was counter to his ambition. She also told him to prepare to return to his real identity; otherwise he would become wicked and unhappy, and she would abandon him to his former troubles.

Rosimond took the fairy's counsel to heart and told everyone that he was going on a secret mission to a neighboring land. He embarked on a vessel that swiftly took him to the island where the fairy had told him he would find the real prince. The savage people who had captured the prince forced him to guard their sheep. Rosimond, becoming invisible, found the prince in the pasture, and, covering him with his invisible mantle, took him to the ship and sailed for home.

When they arrived in the presence of the king, Rosimond confessed that he had posed as the prince. He told the king that he wasn't his son, but that he had brought his real son back to him. The king was astounded and asked who had defeated his enemies and won such a glorious peace. The prince said that it had been Rosimond who had gained the victory and then had set him free from his island captors. He said that he owed his happiness in returning home to Rosimond.

The king could hardly believe his ears until Rosimond turned the ring and appeared to him as the prince. The king offered Rosimond immense rewards, which he refused. The only favor that Rosimond would accept was a place at court for his brother Bramintho. Rosimond feared his own weakness and wanted only to return to his native village and see his mother and cultivate the land.

One day Rosimond was wandering through the woods when he met the fairy, who led him to the cave where his father was imprisoned. She told him the words to set his father free. Rosimond repeated them, for he always intended to bring the old man back and to make his last days happy. After Rosimond had the pleasure of doing good to all those who had wished to do him evil, he resolved to return the ring to the fairy. He feared that if he kept it, he might be tempted to use it for selfish purposes.

While Rosimond tried to give back the ring to the fairy, Bramintho, who had learned nothing from his experiences, attempted to persuade the prince, who had since become king, to mistreat Rosimond. The fairy knew this. When he was imploring her to accept the ring, she warned, "Your wicked brother is doing his best to poison the mind of the king against you and to ruin you. He deserves to be punished, and he must die. In order that he may destroy himself, I will give the ring to him."

Rosimond wept at these words and asked what she meant by giving the ring as a punishment. He argued that his brother would only use it to persecute everyone and to become master.

The fairy told Rosimond, "The same things are often a healing medicine to one person and a deadly poison to another. Prosperity is the source of all evil to a naturally wicked man. If you wish to punish a scoundrel, the first thing to do is to give him power. You will see that with this rope, he will soon hang himself."

The fairy left the woods and went directly to the palace, where she presented herself to Bramintho disguised as an old woman covered with rags. She told him, "I have taken this ring from the hands of your brother, to whom I had lent it, and with its help he covered himself with glory. I now give it to you. Be careful what you do with it."

Bramintho replied with a laugh that he certainly would not imitate his brother, who was foolish enough to bring back the prince instead of reigning in his place. Bramintho was as good as his word. The only use he made of the ring was to discover family secrets and betray them, to commit murders and every other sort of wickedness, and to gain wealth for himself unlawfully. All of these crimes, which could not be traced to anybody, mystified the people.

The king, seeing so many public and private affairs exposed, was at first as puzzled as anyone, until Bramintho's wonderful prosperity and astounding insolence made the king suspect that the ring had become Bramintho's property. To find out the truth, the king bribed a stranger from a nation with whom the he was always at war to sneak in at night to see Bramintho and offer him untold honors and rewards if he would betray state secrets.

Bramintho agreed to everything the stranger proposed and accepted at once the first payment for the crime; however, his triumph was short. The next day he was seized by order of the king and the ring taken from him. He was searched and papers were found on him that proved his guilt. Bramintho was put to death. The ring had been more fatal to him than it had been beneficial in the hands of his brother.

To console Rosimond for the fate of Bramintho, the king gave him the enchanted ring. Rosimond immediately went into the woods looking for the fairy to return the ring. He said to her, "Here is your ring. My brother's experience has made me know many things that I did not know before. Keep it; it has led only to destruction.

"Without it he would be alive now and my father and mother would not be bowed down with shame and grief in their old age. Perhaps he might have been wise and happy if he had never had the chance to gratify his wishes. How dangerous it is to have more power that the rest of the world! Take back your ring. Since ill fortune seems to follow all on whom you bestow it, I implore you never to give it to anyone who is dear to me."

Moral: Power is best used in the hands of the wise and the just.

Based on: Andrew Lang, "The Enchanted Ring,"
   The Green Fairy Book

Chapter 6

RESOLUTE / COURAGEOUS

There is no chance, no destiny, no fate,
Can circumvent or hinder or control
The firm resolve of a determined soul.
Gifts count for nothing; will alone is great;
All things give way before it, soon or late.
What obstacle can stay the mighty force
Of the sea-seeking river in its course,
Or cause the ascending orb of day to wait?
Each well-born soul must win what it deserves.
Let the fool prate of luck. The fortunate
Is he whose earnest purpose never swerves,
Whose slightest action or inaction serves
The one great aim. Why, even Death stands still,
And waits an hour sometimes for such a will.

Ella Wheeler Wilcox, "Will"

The Little Hero of Holland

Much of the land in Holland lies below sea level. Since the level of the land is lower than that of the sea, the water is held back by great walls, called dikes, to keep the North Sea from rushing in and flooding farms and villages. For centuries the Dutch people have worked hard to keep the dikes strong and their land safe. Everyone, including children, watches the walls regularly because a small leak can rapidly grow into a large leak that might cause a disastrous flood.

Years ago a young boy named Peter lived in the city of Haarlem in Holland. Peter's father tended the gates in the dikes, called sluices, which allowed ships to pass between Holland's canals and the North Sea. One autumn day when Peter was eight years old, he walked across the top of the dike near his home to visit his grandmother.

Peter's mother had told him to be home before dark, so he started for home just before sunset. He ran along the top of the dike because he had stayed at his grandmother's cottage longer than he had intended. He realized that he was going to be late for supper. Farmers working in nearby fields had all finished their work and left for home. Peter could hear the waves beating against the great wall. Recent rains had caused the water level to rise.

Suddenly Peter heard a noise—the sound of trickling water. He stopped and looked down the side of the dike to find the source of the noise. He saw a small hole in the dike, through which a thin but steady stream of water was flowing. He realized that it would not take long for the small hole to become a large one. He looked around for something with which to plug the hole, but he could find nothing.

Peter reached down and stuck his forefinger into the tiny hole in the dike, and the flow of water stopped. He called for help as loudly as he could. No one was around to hear, however; everyone was home at supper. Soon night fell, and it became much colder. Peter continued to call out for help. He hoped that someone would walk across the dike that evening to visit a friend. No one came.

Peter's mother looked for him along the dike many times and finally closed and locked the cottage door. She assumed that Peter had decided to stay overnight with his grandmother, as he had done many times. Peter thought of his brother and sister in their warm beds, but he was not going to abandon his responsibility. He did not sleep that night. He was grateful that the moon and stars provided light.

Early the next morning a man walking along the top of the dike on his way to work heard a groan. He looked over the edge of the wall and saw Peter, who was weary and aching from his vigil. He asked Peter if he was hurt. Peter told him that he was holding the water back and asked him to go for help. The alarm was spread, and men came running to repair the hole. Peter was carried home, and the word spread in Haarlem and beyond of the brave little hero of Holland.

Moral: By being responsible and unselfish, an individual can
      protect the many.

Based on: J. Berg Esenwein and Marietta Stockard,
      "The Little Hero of Haarlem,"
      Children's Stories and How to Tell Them

Horatius at the Bridge

At the end of the sixth century BC, the Roman people were at war with the Etruscans who lived on the other side of the Tiber River from Rome. The Etruscan king, Lars Porsena, raised a large army and marched toward Rome, which was a small city then and did not have many fighting men. Rome had never been in such great danger before.

The Romans knew that they were not strong enough to meet the Etruscans in open battle. They stayed inside the walls of the city and posted guards on all approaching roads. One morning Porsena's army was seen coming from the hills in the north. Thousands of horsemen and men on foot were marching toward the wooden Sublician bridge over the Tiber River. The elderly statesmen who governed Rome did not know what to do. They knew if the Etruscan army gained the bridge, it could not be stopped from entering the city.

Among the guards at the bridge was a brave man named Horatius. He was on the other side of the river from the city. When he saw how close the approaching Etruscans were, he called out to the Romans behind him to cut down the bridge. He told them that he and the two men with him would hold back the attacking army. With their shields in front of them and their long spears in their hands, the three men held back the horsemen that Porsena had sent to take the bridge.

The Romans behind them chopped away at the beams and posts supporting the bridge. Their axes rang out, the wood chips flew, and soon the bridge shuddered and was ready to collapse. The men on the bridge called out to Horatius and his two companions to come back across the bridge and save their lives. At that moment, Porsena's horsemen dashed towards them. Horatius told the two guards with him to run for their lives across the bridge while it was still standing. He told them that he would hold the road.

Horatius's companions ran back across the bridge and had barely reached the other side when the sound of crashing beams and timbers could be heard. The bridge toppled over to one side and then fell with a loud splash into the river. When Horatius heard that sound, he knew that the city was safe.

Facing Porsena's men, Horatius moved backward slowly until he was standing on the river bank. A dart thrown by one of the Etruscan soldiers put out his left eye. Still, he did not falter; he cast his spear at the nearest horseman and then quickly turned around. He could see the white porch of his own home among the trees on the other side of the river.

Horatius leaped into the deep, swift river. Wearing his heavy armor, he sank out of sight. No one expected to see him again. Fortunately, he was a strong man and one of Rome's best swimmers. When he came up, he was halfway across the river and out of range of the spears and darts hurled by Porsena's soldiers.

When Horatius reached the other side, his fellow soldiers stood ready to help him up the river bank. The Romans shouted with pride at brave Horatius's accomplishment as he climbed out of the river. The Etruscans cheered too; they had never seen a man as strong and courageous as Horatius. He had kept them out of Rome, but they did not hesitate to praise him.

The Romans were extremely grateful to Horatius for saving their city. They called him Horatius Cocles, which meant "one-eyed Horatius," because he had lost an eye defending the bridge. The city fathers erected a large brass statue in his honor in the

Temple of Vulcan. They awarded him as much land as he could plow around in a single day. For hundreds of years afterward, the people of Rome sang about his bravery in keeping the Etruscans out of their city.

Moral: A determined individual can achieve success in a
　　　　situation that appears hopeless.

Based on: James Baldwin, "Horatius at the Bridge,"
　　　　Favorite Tales of Long Ago

Crossing the Rubicon

In the first century BC, Rome was the most powerful city-state in the world. The Romans had conquered all the countries on the north side of the Mediterranean Sea and most of those on the south side and occupied what is now modern Turkey. Julius Caesar had led a large army into Gaul, the part of Europe that today includes France, Belgium, and Switzerland, and made it a Roman province. He crossed the Rhine River to conquer part of Germany and also established colonies in Britain. He had become the hero of Rome.

For nine years, Caesar had served his republic loyally, but he had enemies at home, those who feared his ambition and envied his achievements. Pompey, the most powerful man in Rome, was one of them. Like Caesar, he commanded a great army, but he had done little to distinguish himself militarily. Pompey made plans to destroy Caesar.

In 49 BC, Caesar's service in Gaul was scheduled to end, and the plan was that he would return to Rome and be elected consul, or ruler, of the Roman republic. Pompey and his supporters were determined to prevent this, so they convinced the Roman Senate to command Caesar to return to Rome, leaving his army in Gaul. Caesar was told that if he didn't obey this order, he would be considered an enemy of the republic. He knew if he did obey it, false accusations would be made against him. He would be tried for treason, and subsequently not be elected consul.

Caesar called his veteran soldiers together and told them about the plot. They declared their loyalty to him and agreed to go with him to Rome, serving without pay, if necessary. The troops started for Rome with enthusiasm, willing to face any danger. They came to the Rubicon River, a small river in north-central Italy that flowed into the Adriatic Sea and marked the boundary between Cisalpine Gaul and Italy.

By law, Roman magistrates could bring armies into Italy only with the permission of the Senate. Crossing the Rubicon River without that permission was a declaration of war against Pompey and the Senate. Caesar would commit himself to a showdown with Rome itself. This action could involve all of Rome in turmoil.

Caesar hesitated on the banks of the Rubicon. He realized that safety was behind him. Once he crossed the Rubicon into Italy, there was no turning back. When he decided to cross, his decision was irrevocable. News of his crossing was passed along the roads leading to Rome. People turned out to welcome the returning hero. The closer he got to Rome, the more enthusiastic were the celebrations.

Caesar encountered no resistance when he and his army marched through the gates of Rome. Pompey and his supporters had fled. The phrase "crossing the Rubicon" has become known as making a decision from which there is no turning back.

Moral: Occasionally, a decision must be made that is truly irrevocable. Much forethought must be given to such a decision.

Based on: James Baldwin, "Crossing the Rubicon,"
Thirty More Famous Stories Retold

Thunder Falls

Two brave Kickapoo women are legendary for their great courage and the noble sacrifice they made for their tribe. The story begins with a band of Kickapoo braves hunting in the early spring, when the green earth was coming out from beneath the snow, and the rivers and streams were running fast. The women accompanied the men to help skin the animals taken in the hunt and to strip and dry the meat. The party had hunted for three days, and many deer had fallen to their arrows.

When they traveled in country far from their own, there was

always danger of attack by their enemies. The braves kept watch, but they did not watch well enough. One day as they were preparing to return to their tribe, a large Shawnee war party surrounded and attacked the camp. The Kickapoo who were not killed or badly wounded escaped down into nearby gorges. When they had hunted there, they had found a great cave beneath the thundering waterfalls of a mighty river. The chief had chosen it as their designated hiding place if they encountered an enemy war party. All the Kickapoo knew of the cave.

The savage Shawnee killed the wounded and took two of the Kickapoo women back to their camp as prisoners who would be made to work. The Shawnee camp was far upriver from the place where the Kickapoo had been attacked. The Shawnee lodges were on the banks of the wide, fast-flowing river. For six days after the attack, the Shawnee warriors searched for the Kickapoo who had escaped the raid. Sentries were placed at distant points so the Kickapoo could not escape without being seen. The Shawnees searched thoroughly but did not discover the Kickapoo hiding place. The Kickapoo did not have to leave the great cavern because they had plenty of dried meat and water.

Nevertheless, after several days the Kickapoo begged the chief to let them leave their shelter beneath the waterfalls. Although the people were safe there, the roaring noise of the falls hurt their ears. Also, they feared that spirits of evil dwelt in the dark, rocky gorges surrounding them. The chief agreed with them and was willing to risk the arrows of the Shawnees to return to their own territory. He decided that after hiding for seven days, they should attempt a night escape. The chief realized that their chances of reaching safety were few because the many Shawnee were angry at not having found the Kickapoo. Fortunately, the best Shawnee trackers were ineffective in the rocky ground of the river gorges.

The Shawnee medicine man went to his chief on the seventh day and told him of a dream he had. His totem bird, the red-tailed hawk, had come to him in a dream and had flown in circles, urging him to follow it. He followed the hawk to a circle of Shadow People in a clearing in the forest. The medicine man asked the hawk if he could follow the Shadow People to the enemy's hiding place. He also asked the hawk if anyone knew of the hiding place, and the hawk led him to the two women prisoners. The medicine man concluded that the women must know, because his hawk totem had never led him astray.

The Shawnee chief had great confidence in his medicine man. The chief called a council of his warriors and told them of the dream. He had the two captive women brought before the council and questioned. They declared that they did not know the location of the surviving Kickapoo. The Shawnees suspected that the women were lying and decided to torture them. Blazing twigs were held to their wrists, and ultimately they cried out that they would reveal the Kickapoo hiding place.

The Shawnees armed themselves and followed the women, who led them to the river. They explained that their people were far away and could be more easily reached by canoe. The chief believed them and took them to the large canoes on the riverbank. The women told them that close to the falls there was a small branch of the river, which they must follow to reach the hidden Kickapoo. The chief ordered the women into the first canoe along with himself, the medicine man, and six of his best warriors. The rest of the party followed closely in many canoes. Paddles flashed, and the canoes moved out into the river.

After paddling awhile, the chief asked if they were getting close to the hiding place. The women said that they were approaching it. The river became swifter, and the braves did not have to paddle as hard. The thunder of the falls could be heard in the distance. The earth-shaking roar came closer and closer. The chief was brave, but even he feared the force of the swiftly rushing waters. He sat directly behind the two women, who were in the bow. He tapped them on the shoulder, and they turned to him at once. His fear ceased when he saw that both women were smiling. The older of the two, with a wave of her arm toward the south bank, pointed out the fork in the river where the paddlers could swing the canoes from the rushing current to the calm water of the smaller stream. The canoes went faster and faster, dashing through the foaming torrent. The rushing river narrowed as it roared between solid walls of rock. The canoes could not be turned.

Too late, the chief and his warriors realized that they had been tricked. Only the bravest had time to sing a few notes of their death song before the canoes were swept over the crest of the mighty waterfall. The two brave Kickapoo women proudly led the band of enemy warriors to their death on the rocks below. Revered by their nation, the women were the subject of stories frequently told around campfires.

Moral: If they are courageous and willing to sacrifice, the few
      can save the many.

Based on: Allan Macfarlan, "Thunder Falls," *Fireside
      Book of North American Indian Folktales*

The Brave Three Hundred

The famous battle of Thermopylae, a Greek pass leading into Thessaly, was fought in 480 BC. King Xerxes of Persia led his army into Greece along the coast between Mount Oeta and the Maliac Gulf. The only route into Greece from the east was through the narrow pass at Thermopylae, named for hot springs nearby.

The pass was guarded by Leonidas, king of the Spartans, with only a few thousand men. They were greatly outnumbered by the Persian army. Leonidas positioned his warriors in the narrowest part of the pass, where a few men armed with long spears could hold off an entire company. The Persian attack began at dawn.

Arrows rained down on the Greek defenders, but their shields deflected them, and their long spears held back the Persians. The invaders attacked again and again with terrible losses. Finally Xerxes sent his best troops, known as the Ten Thousand Immortals, into battle but they fared no better against the determined Greeks.

After two days of fighting, Leonidas still held the pass. That night a Greek who knew the local terrain well was brought into Xerxes's camp. He told Xerxes that the pass was not the only way through. A hunter's footpath wound the long way around, to a trail along the spine of the mountain. It was held by a handful of Greeks who could easily be overcome, and then the Spartan army could be attacked from the rear. The treacherous plan worked, but a few Greeks escaped to warn Leonidas.

The Greeks knew that if they did not abandon the pass at once, they would be trapped. However, Leonidas also realized that he must delay Xerxes longer while the Greeks prepared the defenses of their cities. He made the difficult decision to order most of his troops to slip through the mountains and back to their cities, where they would be needed. He retained three hundred of his Spartans and a small number of Thespians and Thebans and prepared to defend the pass until the end.

Xerxes and his army advanced. The Spartans stood fast, but one by one they fell. When their spears broke, they fought with swords and daggers. All day they kept the Persian army at bay. By sundown, not one Spartan was left alive.

Xerxes had taken the pass, but at a cost of thousands of men and a delay of several days. This delay was critical. The Greeks were able to gather their forces, including their navy, and soon drove the Persians back to Asia. Many years later, a monument was erected at the pass of Thermopylae in memory of the courageous stand of a few in the defense of their homeland.

Moral: The courage of the few can save the many.

Based on: James Baldwin, "The Brave Three Hundred," *Favorite Tales of Long Ago*

Chapter 7

EMPATHETIC / COMPASSIONATE

Unbounded courage and compassion joined,
Tempering each other in the victor's mind,
Alternately proclaim him good and great,
And make the hero and the man complete.

Joseph Addison, *The Campaign*

For Those Without Hope

Once there lived a wealthy man who wanted to give charity to others; however, he was determined to give his money only to those who had lost all hope. He reasoned that only without hope is a person entirely dependent on others and therefore definitely in need of charity.

The wealthy man was walking along the roadside one day when he saw a poor man sitting in the road. The man was dressed in tattered clothing and seemed completely forlorn. The wealthy man thought that at last he had found a person who had lost hope and therefore was worthy of receiving charity. The wealthy man approached the poor man and offered him money, saying, "I'd like to give you this because I see that you have no hope left."

The poor man looked up and said, "You are wrong. I have hope, but you are the one without it." The wealthy man was surprised and expressed shock that a poor man would speak like that to someone who was trying to help him. He asked for an explanation. The poor man asked, "Do you not know how God works? The Holy One, blessed be He, turns the wheel so that the poor shall be given help and the mighty made to fall."

The wealthy man said, "Perhaps you can help me in my search. I am looking for those who have abandoned hope entirely." The poor man replied, "You seek only the dead, for they are the only ones from whom hope is completely gone." The wealthy man was persuaded by the power of the stranger's reasoning and immediately went to a cemetery, where he buried one hundred coins in a grave, offering it to the man at rest there.

Later the wealthy man encountered severe economic hardship. He worked hard, but he couldn't hold on to his money. Soon he lost it all. He did not even have a crust of bread to eat. At the time of his greatest desperation, he remembered the coins that he had buried in the cemetery. He went there to dig up the coins from the grave, but he was discovered. People thought that he was a grave robber who had come to steal the shroud of the deceased. He was arrested and brought before the mayor of the town.

The mayor listened to the accusations of the people and then turned to hear the story from the man standing in front of him. When the accused had finished his story, he concluded, "So you see, I did not plan to steal the shroud at all, only to recover the coins that I had placed there earlier."

The mayor looked at the accused and said, "Perhaps you do not recognize me, sir. I am the poor man who suggested to you that only the dead were without hope. God stayed with me until I rose in life to become mayor. And so, you see, both of us have learned that a person can never rely on money in life. You wanted to give charity to me when you had the means to do so, and now I shall take care of your needs until the end of your days."

Moral: Wealth does not guarantee happiness. One good turn deserves another.

Based on: Lawrence J. Epstein, "For Those Without Hope," *A Treasury of Jewish Inspirational Stories*

The Chest of Broken Glass

Once there was an old widower who lived alone. He had worked hard all his life as a tailor. He lost his savings through misfortune and was so infirm that he could no longer work to support himself. His hands trembled too much to thread a needle, and his vision was too blurred to sew a straight stitch.

The old man had three grown sons who were all married. They were busy with their own lives, and they only had time to visit their father and have dinner with him once a week. Gradually, the old tailor grew more and more feeble, and his sons visited him less and less. He was worried that they wouldn't want to be around him, fearing that he would become a burden. He lay awake one night, thinking about what would become of him, when he thought of a plan.

The next morning the old tailor went to see his friend the carpenter, whom he asked to make a large chest. Then he went to his friend the locksmith and obtained an old lock. Finally he went to see his friend the glassblower and asked him for all the old scraps of broken glass that he had. The old man took the chest home, filled it with the pieces of broken glass, locked it, and placed it under the kitchen table.

The next time his sons came to dinner, they bumped their feet against the chest and asked their father what was in it. He told them that it was just some things he was saving. His sons nudged it and found that it was heavy. They kicked the chest and heard a rattling inside. They concluded that it was full of the gold that their father had saved over the years.

The sons concluded that they should protect the treasure. They decided to take to take turns living with their father. That way they could look after him, too. The first week the youngest son moved in with the old man and cared for and cooked for him. The next week the middle son took his brother's place, and the week after that the oldest son took his turn.

Eventually the old tailor grew sick and died. The sons gave him a nice funeral. With a fortune sitting under the kitchen table, they thought they could afford to splurge on the old man. After the funeral service, they searched the house for the key, found it, and opened the chest.

They were surprised to find it full of broken glass and thought what a cruel thing their father had done to them. When they thought further about it, though, they asked themselves what else could he have done. If it hadn't been for the chest, they would have neglected him until the end of his days.

The youngest son admitted to being ashamed of himself for forcing their father to stoop to deceit, because they had ignored the Commandment that he had taught them when they were young. The oldest son tipped the chest over and emptied it onto the floor to ensure that nothing had been hidden under the glass. The three brothers looked inside the chest and read an inscription that had been left for them on the bottom: Honor thy father and mother.

Moral: Children have responsibilities to their parents as they
       grow old.

Based on: Andrew Lang, "The Chest of Broken Glass,"
     The Book of Romance

The Slandered Sister

There once was a very rich merchant who had two armed guards standing at the gate of his princely mansion and five banners flying over it. After his wife's sudden death, his children, a son and a daughter, were left without a mother's care. The merchant employed a tutor to give them a good education. A special room was set aside in the mansion for the children's lessons. The brother and sister were so attached to each other that they were inseparable.

One day after the merchant had led his caravan back from Istanbul, he called his son, named Simon, to his bedside and said, "I am dying, my son. The end has come for me, but I leave you a great fortune. If you stay idle, you will be a poor man in two years. I worked hard to earn this wealth, but it would be easy for you to squander it. I expect you to follow in my footsteps and to take over my business interests in Istanbul and other cities. When you go to Istanbul, be sure to see my friend Petros Aga. Petros and I are like brothers. He will help you sell your merchandise."

The old merchant passed away. His funeral service was held, and alms were distributed to the poor. After a few weeks of mourning, Simon announced to his sister that he could no longer stay at home doing nothing. He had to buy, to sell, and to keep busy as their father had wanted him to. He told her that he was leaving for Istanbul in a few days. She asked him how she could live at home alone without him. She couldn't stay away from him for even a hour. He answered that it couldn't be helped; he had to go.

The young woman was heartbroken. Simon hired a servant, a reliable woman, he thought, so that his sister wouldn't be alone in the house during his absence. Before he led his father's caravan to Istanbul, he gave his sister his photograph, and she gave him hers.

On reaching Istanbul, Simon went directly to Petros Aga's shop in the bazaar. He informed Petros Aga that his father had died and that he would carry on his father's business. Petros Aga broke down and wept. He had no children of his own, and he and his wife were glad to have a fine, upstanding young man like Simon live with them as an adopted son.

Petros Aga was very rich himself and a personal friend of the king. When he went to the palace for an audience with the king, he took Simon with him. The youth kissed the hand of the king, who said that had known Simon's father and was glad to meet his son. The king's only son took a liking to Simon, and they became close friends. Simon spent most of his time at the palace with the young prince and was his dinner guest almost every day.

One day about a month later, Simon suggested to Petros Aga

that they invite the prince to dinner. Simon admitted that he didn't know how proper it would be, but that he had enjoyed the prince's hospitality for a month. Petros Aga said that it was an excellent idea, and that he would make the necessary arrangements. Simon mustered the courage to invite the prince to dinner, and the prince responded that he would like to come.

Petros Aga had the streets between his mansion and the royal palace covered with expensive carpets, and the prince arrived with the vizier and two palace guards in front of him and two guards behind him. Petros Aga served a royal dinner, sparing no expense. The prince enjoyed his visit, and when it was time for him to go, Simon suggested that he sleep in Petros Aga's house that night. The prince agreed, and the youths told jokes and laughed until bedtime.

The crown prince, the vizier, and Simon went to bed in the same room. The photograph of the beautiful girl hanging on the wall attracted the attention of the prince and the vizier, particularly when they saw Simon glance at it frequently. They said nothing, but that photograph kept the prince up all night.

The next morning when the prince got dressed, he looked sad and thoughtful. Simon asked what was wrong and whether he had said anything to offend the prince. The prince answered that, as close as they were as friends, he didn't think that Simon kept secrets from him.

Simon assured the prince that he had no secrets from him. The prince asked Simon had never mentioned the young woman whose photograph was on the wall of Simon's bedroom. The prince said that he had seen Simon look at the photograph. If the young woman meant so much to Simon, the prince would do anything to help him marry her. Simon exclaimed that she was his sister.

At that moment, love for Simon's sister blazed in the heart of the prince. He could not even eat his breakfast; he just drank a cup of tea. His vizier was smitten, too, but said nothing.

The prince returned to the palace a sick young man. His mother put him to bed, but he wouldn't tell her what ailed him. The king hastened to his son's bedside with his advisors and his physicians. The doctors were puzzled by the prince's illness and didn't know how to treat it. The patient got worse. Everyone was worried. The prince was the idol of Istanbul; the entire city was grief-stricken.

The prince's mother told him that he had been in perfectly good health when he went to his friend's house for dinner. She begged him to tell her what had happened. Finally, the prince told his mother that he would kill himself if he couldn't marry Simon's sister. The queen reminded him that he was the king's son, and the girl was only a merchant's daughter.

The queen asked him if he wouldn't be ashamed to marry a commoner. How would the king react, and what would the people think? She argued that there were many royal princesses he could marry. The prince replied that Simon's sister was the only girl for him; he could not live without her.

The queen went to the king and explained that their son was in love with Simon's sister and had threatened to kill himself if he couldn't marry her. The king asked how he could be expected to humiliate himself by requesting the hand of a merchant's daughter. The queen told the king that she had asked the same question.

Simon and Petros Aga were summoned to the palace. The king told Simon that the prince was in love with his sister and asked if this met with his approval. Simon and Petros Aga didn't think the king was serious. When the king assured them that he wasn't joking, Simon answered that the prince was his best friend, and that he would gladly agree to his sister's marriage to the prince.

After receiving permission to marry Simon's sister, the prince got well. The king proclaimed a holiday and ordered his subjects to celebrate his son's recovery and forthcoming marriage. Everyone was happy except the vizier, who was determined to prevent the marriage. He reasoned that with the competition out of the way, he could marry the young woman himself. He reported to the king that he had heard that Simon's sister was a common tramp, and that she had at least twenty lovers.

The king was furious. He sent for Simon and Petros Aga to demand an explanation. He threatened to have them hung for deceiving him and asked if they expected his son to marry someone with such a reputation. The king rebuked Simon for knowing what his sister was when he gave his consent. Simon and Petros Aga were stunned.

"May the king live long," Simon said at last, "If my sister is such a bad woman, hang me! But if it is a lie, then I hope that you hang her slanderer!"

Simon and Petros signed a statement dictated by the king. If the accusation proved to be true, they were destined for the gallows. The king agreed to investigate. The vizier asked the king for thirty days to prove his claim or the king could hang him if he lied.

The vizier rode off to see Simon's sister. The guards at the mansion's gate asked him to identify himself. He said that he was a friend of their master from Istanbul, and that he had a letter from him for his sister. The guards told their mistress about the man who claimed to have a letter from her brother. She told them not to let him in until she saw the letter. Her brother had told her to be very careful and not to admit any strangers.

Simon's sister read the vizier's letter and realized that it wasn't written by her brother. She ordered the guards to give the letter back to the man, send him away, and tell him that if he tried to set foot in her house, he would regret it.

The vizier was sorely disappointed, so he attempted another approach—bribing the young woman's servant. The old woman pocketed a handful of gold coins and promised to bring the vizier a token from her mistress.

The old woman helped her mistress with her daily bath in a marble pool. As the girl undressed, she took off her ring, placed it on her clothes, and asked the servant to put them away. The old woman brought fresh clothes after the girl had her bath, but she slipped the ring into her own pocket. The young woman forgot to put on the ring after her bath. It never occurred to her that her servant would steal it.

The ring was worth a king's ransom, and the vizier was very happy to have it. He rewarded the servant with another handful of coins and raced back to Istanbul. The next day, Simon's sister noticed that her ring was missing. She turned the house upside down but could not find it. The old servant would not confess her theft and swore that she was innocent. The young woman suspected that the stranger had something to do with the missing ring.

The vizier gave the stolen ring to the king and said, "I told you what she was, but you would not believe me. Well, I made love to her, and she gave me this ring as a token of her affection for me."

Simon and Petros Aga were summoned to the palace. The king received them in the great council chamber. He handed the ring to Simon and asked if it was his sister's ring. Simon examined at it and replied that it was his sister's ring. The king told them that he intended to hang both of them for deceiving him. He told them that Simon's sister had given the ring to the vizier along with other favors bestowed upon him.

"May the king live long," said Simon. "Grant us five days before you hang us." The king granted their request.

Simon drove home with Petros in a fast carriage. The guards at the gate were happy to see their master again, but he would not go into the house. He told them to ask his sister to come out, because he had something important to tell her. She came out of the house to embrace her brother, but he would not even look at her. "For shame!" he cried and spat in her face. Then the two men drove off without saying another word.

The sister connected one thing to another and realized that she had to move fast to save her brother. She hurried to the bazaar and bought another ring like the one that had been stolen from her. She appealed to the influential men in the city, and they signed a statement vouching for her reputation and character. She hired a carriage and told the driver to drive her to Istanbul as fast as he could.

Simon's sister left the carriage on the outskirts of the city, paid the driver, pulled her long silk mantle over her head, and entered an Armenian church. She stood beside a woman who was wept as she prayed. She asked the woman what she was crying about. The woman sobbed that they were going to hang her husband the next day with a merchant's son who had been living with them, all because of the boy's sister, a shameless hussy. The woman then identified herself as Petros Aga's wife.

Simon's sister said that she had just arrived in Istanbul and didn't know a soul. Petros Aga's wife agreed that the young woman could stay at her house, and then she confided the rest of the story.

The next morning, Petros Aga's wife and Simon's sister heard the bugles blowing, announcing the hanging. Simon and Petros Aga were led through the marketplace in prison garb, with the royal decree ordering their execution pinned to their chests. There was loud wailing in the home of Petros Aga, and Simon's sister tried to comfort Petros Aga's wife, reminding her that God was merciful.

The young woman drew her mantle around herself and ran to the public square where the gallows had been erected. The noose was already around her brother's neck. The crowd made way for her as she hurried up to the king, who wanted to see the hanging with his own eyes. The angry monarch saw standing before him a beautiful girl, whose face seemed familiar.

The girl said, "May the king live long; I have a complaint."

The king asked what her complaint was.

The young woman said, "Please don't hang these two men until you hear my story. Then you can decide what to do with them, and with me."

The king ordered the hangman to wait. Simon's sister took the new ring out of her pocket and told the king that she had another ring just like it, which his vizier had stolen by bribing her servant.

"My vizier! Stole your ring!" The king couldn't believe his ears. The vizier's heart stopped beating. "Did you steal that ring?" the king asked his chamberlain. "Is she telling the truth?"

The vizier's knees were shaking. "May the king live long. I don't know the girl; I never saw her before in my life."

"You heard him!" she cried. "He never saw me before, but he says he made love to me! Oh, my king, if your vizier told you the truth about me, then I am the guilty one, and you should hang me, not two innocent men."

The king encouraged her to continue. All his counselors heard the girl with murmurs and exclamations of horror and surprise. A hush fell over the great throng gathered in the square. Simon's sister told the king how the vizier had come to her house with a false letter from her brother, and how he had bribed her servant to steal the ring.

Then she took a paper from her bosom and handed it to the king. It bore the signatures of all the great men of her city. The king read aloud, "We can vouch for this girl's character. We do not know of a more decent, upright maiden in our city. She is blameless of any wrong. All of us hold her in high esteem." The king ordered that the two prisoners be immediately released. The vizier was strung up in their place.

The wedding of Simon's sister to the prince was celebrated for forty days and forty nights. Everyone said that the bride was the prettiest and wisest maiden in the region. The entire city rejoiced in their happiness.

Moral: "There is nothing that more betrays a base, ungenerous
        spirit than the giving of secret stabs to a man's [or a
        woman's] reputation." Joseph Addison, *The Spectator*

Based on: Leon Surmelian, "Slandered Sister,"
        Apples of Immortality: Folktales of Armenia

Reconciliation by Courier

It was neither the season nor the hour when the park was busy. It
was likely that the young lady seated on a bench along the walkway
merely had an impulse to sit a while and enjoy a foretaste of spring.
She rested there, pensive and still. A certain melancholy that
touched her face must have occurred recently, because it had not
changed the youthful lines of her cheek nor the curve of her lips.

A tall young man walked rapidly through the park along the
path near the young lady's bench. A young boy carrying a suitcase
tagged along behind him. When the young man saw the young lady,
his face turned to red and then back to pale. As he drew nearer, he
watched her face with hope and anxiety mingled on his own. He
passed within a few yards of her, but he saw no evidence that she
was aware of his existence.

Fifty yards further along, the young man stopped and sat on a
bench. The boy dropped the suitcase and stared at him with curious,
shrewd eyes. The young man took out his handkerchief and wiped
his brow. He said to the boy, "I want you to take a message to the
young lady on that bench. Tell her that I am on my way to San
Francisco, where I shall join an Alaska moose-hunting expedition.
Tell her that, since she has commanded me neither to speak nor to
write to her, I take this means of making one last appeal to her sense
of justice, for the sake of what has been. Tell her that to condemn
and discard one who has not deserved such treatment, without giving him her reasons or a chance to explain, is contrary to her nature
as I believe it to be. Tell her that I have thus, to a certain degree,
disobeyed her injunctions, in the hope that she may yet be inclined
to see justice done. Go, and tell her that."

The young man placed a silver dollar into the boy's hand. The
boy looked at him with bright, canny eyes in a dirty face and then
set off running. He approached the lady on the bench a little cau-

tiously but unembarrassed. He touched the brim of the old baseball cap perched on the back of his head. She looked at him coolly.

"Lady," he said, "that gent on the other bench sent you a song and dance by me. If you don't know the guy and he is trying to be forward, say the word, and I'll call a cop. If you do know him, and he's on the square, I'll tell you the bunch of hot air he sent you."

The young lady showed a faint interest.

"A song and dance!" she said in a deliberate, sweet voice that clothed her words in barely disguised irony. "I used to know the gentleman who sent you, so I think it would hardly be necessary to call the police. You may do your song and dance, but do not sing too loudly. It is a little early for outdoor entertainment, and we might attract attention."

The boy said, "He told me to tell you that he's got his clothes packed in that suitcase for a trip to Frisco. Then he's going moose hunting in Alaska. He says you told him not to send around any more notes or to come hanging over the garden gate, and he takes this means of putting you wise. He says that you treated him like a referee ejecting someone without allowing him a chance to question the decision. He said that you never explained why."

The slight interest in the young lady's eyes did not change. Perhaps it was caused by either the originality or the audacity of the moose hunter, in getting around her express commands against ordinary means of communication. She replied, "Tell the gentleman that I do not need to repeat to him a description of my ideals. He knows what they have been and what they still are. Absolute loyalty and truth are the most important ones that bear on this case. Tell him that I have studied my own heart, and I know its weaknesses as well as its needs. That is why I do not want to hear his pleas. I do not condemn him because of gossip or questionable evidence, and that is why I made no accusations. You may convey the substance of the matter.

"Tell him that I entered the conservatory that evening from the rear to cut roses for my mother. Tell him I saw him and Miss Ashburton beneath the pink oleander. The scene was pretty, but the pose and the close approximation to each other required no further explanation. I left the conservatory and, at the same time, my ideal. You may carry that song and dance to your impresario."

The gravel spun from beneath the boy's feet, he soon stood by the other bench. The man's eyes interrogated him, hungrily. The boy's eyes were shining with the impersonal zeal of a translator.

"The lady says that gals don't like it when a fellow tells ghost stories to try and make up. She won't listen to any soft soap. She says that she caught you dead to rights hugging a bunch of calico in the hothouse. She had come in to pick some posies, when she found you squeezing the other gal to beat the band. She says it looked cute, but it made her sick. She says you might as well head for the railroad station to board your train."

The young man gave a low whistle and his eyes flashed with a sudden thought. He reached into his pocket and withdrew a letter. He handed it to the boy along with another silver dollar.

"Give that letter to the lady," he said, "and ask her to read it. Tell her that it should explain the situation. Tell her, if she had mingled a little trust with her conception of the ideal, much heartache might have been avoided. Tell her that the loyalty she prizes so much has never wavered. Tell her I am waiting for an answer."

The messenger stood before the lady.

"The gent says that he has been treated unfairly for no reason. He says that he is not a bad guy, and if you read this letter, you will agree that he is a sport."

The young lady unfolded the letter and read it.

Dear Dr. Arnold

,   I want to thank you for your most kind and opportune aid to my daughter last Friday evening, when she was over come by an attack of her old heart trouble in the conservatory at Mrs. Waldron's reception. Had you not been near to catch her as she fell and to render proper attention, we might have lost her. I would be glad if you would call to undertake the treatment of her case.

Gratefully yours,

Robert Ashburton

The young lady refolded the letter and handed it to the boy.

"The gent wants an answer," said the boy. "What's the word?"

The lady's eyes suddenly flashed on him, bright, smiling, and wet. "Tell that guy on the other bench," she said, with a tremulous laugh, "that his girl wants him."

Moral: Things aren't always what they seem. It is worth taking the time to verify impressions, without letting pride get in the way.

Based on: O. Henry, "By Courier," *The Four Million*

The Service of Love

When one loves one's Art, no service seems too hard. Joe Larrabee came out of the plains of the Midwest pulsing with a genius for pictorial art. As six he drew a picture of a prominent citizen of his town. It was framed and hung in the drugstore window. At twenty he left for New York without much money in his pocket. Delia Caruthers did things in six octaves so promisingly in her hometown in the South that her relatives chipped in enough for her to go "North" and "Finish."

Joe and Delia met in a studio where art and music students had gathered to discuss Wagner, music, Rembrandt's works, pictures, and Chopin. Joe and Delia fell in love and in a short time were married. Mr. and Mrs. Larrabee began housekeeping in an apartment. They were happy. They had their Art, and they had each other.

Joe painted in the class of the great Magister, a well-known artist. Magister's fees were high; his lessons were light. Delia studied with Rosenstock, a famous pianist. Joe and Delia were happy as long as their money lasted. When one loves one's Art, no service seems too hard—their aims were clear and defined. Joe was to become capable very soon of turning out pictures that old gentlemen with thin side-whiskers would fall over one another to buy. Delia was to become so accomplished that the concert halls in which she performed would have no unsold seats.

Their home life was happy with ardent chats after the day's study, cozy dinners, and an exchange of ambitions interwoven with the other's help and inspiration. Unfortunately, after a while Art flagged. Everything was going out, and nothing was coming in. Money was lacking to pay their teachers' fees.

When one loves one's Art, no service seems too hard. So, Delia said that she must give music lessons to help pay the rent. For several days, she went out looking for pupils. Finally, she told Joe that she had found a pupil, the daughter of General Pinckney on Seventy-first Street. She described the splendid house where the Pinckneys lived. She had never seem anything like it.

Delia's pupil was the general's eighteen-year-old daughter, Clementina, a delicate thing with simple manners. Delia would give three lessons a week at five dollars a lesson. When she found more pupils, she would be able to resume her lessons with Herr Rosenstock. Delia said that she didn't mind it, and that Joe should smooth out the wrinkle in his brow.

Joe said that it was fine for her, but what about him? He didn't want her hustling for wages while he struggled in the regions of high art. He could sell newspapers or find something to bring in needed money. Delia told him to keep on with his studies, and that it wasn't as though she had given up music. She could learn while she taught, and they could live on fifteen dollars a week. He must not think of leaving Mr. Magister. Joe agreed with her but hated for her to be giving lessons. It wasn't Art, but she was a dear to do it. Delia said, "When one loves one's Art, no service seems too hard."

Joe told her that Magister had praised a sketch that he had made in the park. Also, Tinkle had given him permission to hang two of his sketches in the window of his gallery. Joe hoped to sell one if the right person saw them. Delia told her husband that she was sure he would sell one, but for now they should be thankful to General Pinckney for their veal roast.

During the next week, the Larrabees had early breakfasts. Joe was enthusiastic about some early morning sketches he was doing in Central Park, and Delia sent him off at seven o'clock. Art was an engaging mistress. It was usually seven o'clock when he returned in the evening. At the end of the week, Delia proudly tossed three five-dollar bills on the table.

"Sometimes," she said, a little wearily, "Clementina tires me. She doesn't practice enough, and I have to tell her the same things over and over. Nevertheless, I am really getting attached to her; she is so gentle and well-bred. General Pinckney is the dearest old man. I wish you could meet him. He comes in sometimes when Clementina is at the piano and stands there listening and pulling on his white goatee. General Pinckney's brother was once the Minister to Bolivia."

Joe laid down eighteen dollars alongside Delia's three fives. He announced that he had sold his watercolor of an obelisk to a man from Peoria. Delia asked Joe if he was kidding—a man from Peoria? Joe said that he wished she could have seen him, a fat man with a woolen muffler and a quill toothpick. He had seen the sketch in Tinkle's window and had gone in and bought it. Then the man ordered another one—an oil sketch of the Lackawanna freight depot—to take back with him. Delia responded that she was glad that Joe had kept on with his art, and that he was bound to succeed.

The following Saturday evening, Joe returned home first. He spread his eighteen dollars on the table and washed what appeared to be a great deal of dark paint from his hands. Half an hour later, Delia arrived, her right hand tied up in a shapeless bundle of cloth and bandages. Joe asked what had happened.

Delia explained that Clementina had insisted on a Welsh rarebit after her lesson. It was the servants' day off, so the general had helped her. As Clementina was serving the rarebit, she spilled a lot of it, boiling hot, over Delia's hand and wrist. Delia said that it hurt awfully and Clementina was so sorry; the general himself ran down to the pharmacy for some balm and bandages. Joe asked what the white strands under the bandages were. Delia told him that it was something soft that had oil on it.

Delia saw the money on the table and asked Joe if he had sold another painting. He answered that the man from Peoria picked up his depot painting today, and that he wanted another parkscape and a view of the Hudson River. Joe asked Delia what time she burned her hand.

"Five o'clock, I think," said Delia plaintively. "The iron—I mean the rarebit—came off the fire about that time. You should have seen General Pinckney when . . ."

Joe asked Delia to sit down next to him on the couch. He put his arm around her. Then he asked her what she had been doing for the last two weeks. She was brave for a moment or two while mumbling something about General Pinckney. Then her head went down, and the truth came out, accompanied by tears.

"I couldn't get any pupils," she confessed. "And I couldn't bear to have you give up your lessons. I got a place ironing shirts in the big Twenty-fourth Street laundry. And I think I did very well to make up both General Pinckney and Clementina, don't you, Joe? And when a girl in the laundry set a hot iron down on my hand this afternoon, I thought up the story about the Welsh rarebit on the way home. You're not angry, Joe? And if I hadn't gotten the work, you might not have sold your sketches to that man from Peoria."

Joe answered that there wasn't a man from Peoria. Delia said that it didn't matter where the man was from. Then she asked how he suspected that she wasn't giving music lessons to Clementina.

"I didn't," said Joe, "until tonight. And I wouldn't have then, only I sent up this cotton waste and oil from the engine room this afternoon for a girl upstairs who had her hand burned with a smoothing iron. I've been firing the engine in that laundry for the last two weeks."

"And then you didn't—"

"My purchaser from Peoria," said Joe, "and General Pinckney are both creations of the same Art—but you wouldn't call it either painting or music."

As they both laughed, Joe began, "When one loves one's Art, no service seems . . ."

But Delia stopped him with her hand on his lips. "No," she said," just 'When one loves.'"

Moral: Giving is better than receiving, particularly when compassion motivates one to give something that one treasures.

Based on: O. Henry, "A Service of Love," *The Four Million*

Epilogue

The ultimate value of great legends lies in their inspiring poetry,
Their moral values and their attitude to life.
It is poetically right for the blinded Samson to bring down
The pillars of the Philistine temple upon his enemies and himself,
For Robert Bruce to learn a lesson in resolution from the spider,
For Roland in his obdurate pride to sound the great horn too late
  at Rencesvals,
For the glory of Arthur and his champions of the Round Table
To end in betrayal, destruction and bitter grief.
In legend courage, loyalty, generosity, and greatness of heart
Are upheld against cowardice, treachery, meanness and
  poorness of spirit.
The lesson which the supreme heroes of legend and history have
  to teach is that life need not be petty,
That existence can be vivid, exciting, and intense,
That the limits of human reach and achievement are
Not as narrow and restricted as they so often seem.

Richard Cavendish, *Legends of the World*

Notes

Many of these legends and tales have been passed down by story-tellers and have evolved in the telling. The author gratefully acknowledges the works of other authors, including those from earlier eras, such as James Baldwin (1841-1925), Jesse Lyman Hurlbut (1843-1930), and Andrew Lang (1844-1912), who preserved our heritage and whose endeavors provided many of the stories presented here. These legends and tales have been rewritten to provide a consistent writing style.

Vector art is from IMSI's MasterClips Collection, 1895 Francisco Blvd. East, San Rafael, CA 94901-5506

Bibliography

Baldwin, James. *Favorite Tales of Long Ago*. New York: Dutton, 1955.

—. *Thirty More Famous Stories Retold*. New York: American Book, 1905.

Barnard, Mary. *The Mythmakers*. Athens, Ohio: Ohio University Press, 1966.

Becquer, Gustavo Adolfo. *Romantic Legends of Spain*. New York: Thomas Y. Crowell, 1909.

Bennett, William, ed. *The Book of Virtues*. New York: Simon & Schuster, 1993.

—. *The Moral Compass: Stories for a Life's Journey*. New York: Simon & Schuster, 1995

Bierlein, J. F. *Parallel Myths*. New York: Ballantine Books, 1994.

Bruford, Alan, and Donald A. MacDonald, eds., *Scottish Traditional Tales*. Edinburgh: Polygon, 1994.

Bulfinch, Thomas. *Bulfinch's Mythology*. London: Spring Books, 1967.

Calvino, Italo, ed. *Italian Folktales*. New York: Harcourt Brace Jovanovich, 1956.

Cavendish, Richard. *Legends of the World*. New York: Schocken Books, 1982.

Clouston, W. A. *Popular Tales and Fictions, vols. 1 & 2*. Edinburgh: William Blackwood, 1887.

Colum, Padraic. *Orpheus: Myths of the World*. New York: Gramercy Books, 1993.

Dixon-Kennedy, Mike. *The Robin Hood Handbook: The Outlaw in History, Myth, and Legend*. New York: Sutton, 2006.

Elliot, Alexander. *The Global Myths: Exploring Primitive, Pagan, Sacred, and Scientific Mythologies*. New York: Continuum, 1993.

Epstein, Lawrence J. *A Treasury of Jewish Inspirational Stories*. Northvale, NJ: Jason Aronson, 1993.

Esenwein, J. Berg, and Marietta Stockard. *Children's Stories and How to Tell Them*. Springfield, MA: Home Correspondence School, 1919.

Gibson, Katherine. *The Golden Bird and Other Stories*.

New York: Macmillan, 1927.

Goodrich, Norma Lorre. *Myths of the Hero*. New York: Orion Press, 1958.

Harrell, John and Mary, eds. *A Storytellers Treasury*. New York: Harcourt, 1977.

Hawthorne, Nathaniel. *The Wonder Book*. New York: Franklin Watts, 1963.

Henry, O. *The Four Million*. Garden City: Doubleday, 1906.

The Holy Bible. New York: The Douay Bible House, 1945.

Hoogasian-Villa, Susie, ed. *100 Armenian Tales and Their Folkloristic Relevance*. Detroit: Wayne State University Press, 1966.

Hurlbut, Jesse Lyman. *Hurlbut's Story of the Bible for the Young and Old*. New York: Holt, 1957.

Irving, Washington. *The Alhambra: Tales and Sketches of the Moors and Spaniards*. New York: A. L. Burt, 1924.

Kite, Patricia. *Noah's Ark: Opposing Viewpoints*. San Diego: Greenhaven Press, 1989.

Klees, Emerson. *Legends and Stories of the Finger Lakes Region*. Rochester, NY: Friends of the Finger Lakes Publishing, 1995.

Lang, Andrew, ed. *The Book of Romance*. London: Longmans, Green, 1902

—. *The Crimson Fairy Book*. London: Longmans, Green, 1947.

—. *The Green Fairy Book*. New York: Dover, 1965.

—. *The Lilac Fairy Book*. New York: Dover, 1968.

—. *The Olive Fairy Book*. London: Longmans, Green, 1949.

—. *The Orange Fairy Book*. New York: Dover, 1968.

—. *The Pink Fairy Book*. New York: Dover, 1967.

—. *The Violet Fairy Book*. London: Longmans, Green, 1947.

Lee, F. H. *Folk Tales of All Nations*. New York: Tudor Publishing, 1930.

Mabie, Hamilton Wright. *Heroes Every Child Should Know*. New York: Doubleday, Page, 1906.

Macfarlan, Allan A. *Fireside Book of North American Folktales*. Harrisburg, PA: Stackpole Books, 1974.

Rugoff, Milton, ed. *A Harvest of World Folk Tales*. New York: Viking Press, 1949.

Surmelian, Leon. *Apples of Immortality: Folktales of Armenia*. Berkeley: University of California Press, 1968.

Thompson, Stith, ed. *One Hundred Favorite Folktales.* Bloomington, IN: Indiana University Press, 1968.
Woods, Ralph L., ed. *A Treasury of the Familiar.* New York: Macmillan, 1943.